Covid Express

Norman Pen

Table of Contents

« I »

I read a book recently which embraced the premiss: 'that it all began with Cecily Neville.'

Oddly enough I also wrote one which said much the same thing. Conversely, this story might take a view on microns, and then progress to pathogens and antigens, before laying bacilli to one side in order to shake out a virus. Now I know some millennials like to solve crosswords and others are equally absorbed by Sudoku, but if I'm honest I much prefer to relax with a good paradox; so here for example we might have followed the paper trail of German writer Thomas Mann, who quite uncomplicatedly spoke of 'the genius of disease,' even in the midst of its animus. But in these extraordinary days with the beast in our midst, it's neither paper nor paradox which will avail; direct action alone will defeat it. I should also add that only radical solutions need apply, for until the first vaccines arrived offering temporary respite, the authorities in our respective nations had occupied themselves by making an utter bloater of collaring everybody's unfavourite peste.

And this leads me to the true beginning of this story, when my girlfriend from Italy contacted me just before they were going into lockdown to say how fearful she was of the impending new plague descending upon them and asking for my help. Obviously, this was some time before we had started to take the matter seriously in this country and viewed the Italian response as either characteristically hysterical, or dismissed it, sniffily, as entirely predictable in a land where a slum with a canal rat as sitting tenant is regarded as 'des res.' And why me? - other than my natural concern for her welfare I had no practical experience of health matters whatsoever, let alone any understanding of the complexities of virology. True, our publishers had a strong social media presence that could be exploited, but if I gave the matter any serious thought, I would very soon arrive at the conclusion that social media was exactly the sort of exposure that we could do without.

It soon transpired that it wasn't me in person that she wanted at all, (I trusted the closer relationship remained untainted) but only to use me as a go-between. The real reason was because she knew that our working group included one Verna Slant, a young and brilliant new research assistant recently recruited, and more to the point, a protege of the well-known and powerful investigative TV journalist, Philomena Cnuk. (pronounced nuke) The idea being that if we were to all direct our collective energies to Virus liquidation, we might solve the Covid headache once and for all.

With all the cafes on the sidewalks still looking like isolation sanctuaries I arranged a 'one to one' with Verna to ascertain her thoughts, agreeing to meet at the graveside of Emily Pankhurst in Brompton cemetery, a popular hovering spot for habitues and a would-be shrine for those who would pay their respects to prominent Titanesses in the struggle for sex equality.

It was a clear sunny day I remember, as perfect as if it had been distilled from the morning dew of a Capital city which had lost its desire for commuters and traffic. However, what made it particularly memorable was a perceptible frisson of anticipation in the air as I reflected on the prospect of a pestilence insidious enough to menace such an idyll that could now be now on the verge of utter destruction; such was my confidence in the team behind this post-millennial 'Joan of Arc,' who I knew would dedicate herself to this end. The breeze radiated the first warmth of Spring, so might I be forgiven for getting ahead of myself? For ultimately, how could the world not fete this warrior who I felt sure would give no quarter in crushing the enemy which was threatening the future of the whole human race? Entire Nobel convocations would need to dis-establish in honour of she who transcended their unworthy consideration. I would naturally disclaim any personal credit for any of this. Any woos can stand by the coffee dispenser at Mission Control waving his notebook of Quantum equations, but it's the guy in the capsule, who's getting down deep and dirty, with a one-way ticket to oblivion.

I had only met Verna once before, in the days before the 'V,' when we had attended the same open house organised by the network of publishers to which we both subscribed. Even from a distance I recognised her slim frame coming towards me; she'd forgone the thick camel snorkel by now, in deference to the warmer weather, but still retained the long-sleeved Uniqlo shirt inside the lamb's wool waistcoat, slick blue jeans diving down into brown calf-length boots. None of which defined her half as much as the unique rolling gait of a walk she had about her, shoulder-bag clasped tight to one side, as if to assist with balance. The dark glasses must have limited her field of vision because we had almost transgressed social distancing limits before she recognised me. Virtually close enough to embrace, were we in happier times.

I indicated an empty bench and we book-ended it; she took out her phone and waved it about.

'Notes, 'was all she said. I had texted her the day before, so she knew the purpose of today's meet, essentially to agree a methodology. However, I still felt I needed to tell her what had sparked my interest.

'I know everyone's hacked off by this thing,' I said, 'and we're all done down one way or the other, but I had a call from Anna As in Italy the other day; in fact, you met her at that symposium in Piedmont last summer. They've had the worst of it this year; she, and millions like her, work the local cottage industries which feed their 'haute couture.' Unlikely as it sounds, she's actually a carpenter, but it's the same for seamstresses and button-holers; their jobs have been all but blown away by the virus. If they haven't crashed already, they most certainly will if this damned thing can't be zapped.'

'It's a fact Daly,' said Verna, 'we have to reach beyond these so-called experts, all of whom now call themselves 'scientists,' and think way outside the play pen. Cluster muppets is what Philomena calls them. One she interviewed dissed her out of hand when she suggested he miniaturise himself so he could be injected into a victim's vein and kill it head on. You'd think he'd never heard of 'Fantastic Voyage.' Do you realise that more people can still catch Covid while waiting for their test results than even inside a failed Care-Home full of twirlies off hospital trolleys? Of course, the best solution would be for one total rave going on until next year, but unfortunately most of the elderly would probably object, or die or something, which rather defeats the object.'

'That's why she told me to look you up,' I enthused, 'so you can help us get rid of it. Like I explained, we're here to look at some of the options; any preferences at this stage?'

'Well, I'm definitely not doing that 'pis aller' time machine you've got in your back-room,' she admonished, 'I reckon even Alicia Keys' would be safer than that contraption.'

As a matter of fact, it was not one of the alternatives I had in mind, mainly as we had not yet developed the precision to fix its direction of travel; at the same time, I didn't want to discourage her from any of the more 'outre' solutions which I'd prepared. As it turned out, I needn't have worried.

'And even shrinking to the size of a microbe and chasing it round the block would be against my better judgement, especially as the last bloke who tried it got eaten by a cat.'

I knew who she meant, though it was not strictly true. It was from one of those '50's Sci-Fi 'B'-pictures, in which the house cat had kicked the eponymous shrunken one down into the basement and everyone had just forgotten about him. Intrigued, I let her continue.

'I, that is we, thought: - why not take matters to the other extreme? From the infinitesimal to the infinite.'

'You mean make yourself as big as possible?'

'No, mould wrap, I mean go to the nearest black hole and corner it there.'

'That could be dangerous,' I cautioned.

'D, this virus is a danger to the entire world; destroying it utterly needs more than a battery of toy soldiers. Remember we're only finally rid of it once Covid's progenitor has been cornered and we have shown it no mercy.'

'Very well,' I said, 'then let's have a look at the possibilities, maybe flesh it out a bit?' In fact, my team had looked at this very possibility, but the consensus had been it would be too hard to find a black hole in the dark of outer space. Nonetheless, I kept an open mind.

'The big advantage of a black hole,' said Verna, 'is that you're guaranteed to find the virus; it's bound to be lurking somewhere deep inside because that's where everything in the galaxy ends up eventually. Like there's no escape.'

You could only stand back in awe of this young girl and wonder at her determination and formidable logic; she was on a mission, and if this meant confronting dangers which you and I would baulk at for the benefit of mankind, then there was no doubt in my mind that she was up for it. But did she really understand what the experience would entail?

'I suppose you know how massive a black hole is inside; looking for this particular bacillus would be harder than looking for an anti-social quark. Think how far you might have to penetrate; beyond the singularity gravity compresses matter into zero space, including you and the virus.'

'Oh, we've been reading up on all that,' replied Verna defiantly, 'Stephen Hawking said you'd get pushed back by radiation before you got anywhere near the bottom, like getting your feet too near an electric fire. Anyway, I can run a check on the way in, because he also said you'd also find it licking round the edges. Obviously, I'd be wearing anorak and gloves as protection, probably take a woolly along as well in case it got nippy.'

I was impressed by the depth of their research; perhaps their idea wasn't so far-fetched after all. Even so, there was still one obvious drawback.

'I suppose you know that the nearest black hole is over a thousand light years away?'

'The ones in the sky are, any fule know that. To do this we're going to have to make up our own, or rather you are. Division of labour D, I'm going to be the one going inside of it, doing the virus pulverising bit, it's only fair that you put it together.'

'How do you expect me to make up a black hole?' I asked, taken aback, I certainly hadn't expected such an assignation to be directed my way.

'Build one of course.'

'I wouldn't know where to start.'

'Well look it up on the internet. God, it's not rocket science! You have to start by building a special shed and put it in there; I don't know, have a look round Ikea or something. Come on D, how hard can it be?'

'Look Verna, I can give you the Quantum equations to turn a black hole inside out and even plan a way through one for you so you come out the other side, but I can't build a bookcase, let alone a shed with a black hole inside.'

'I tell you what,' she said condescendingly, 'I know there's a video on You tube which shows you how to do it; then all you have to do is go out and buy all the necessary parts. Here.'

And she shoved her phone over to me: 'Just click on that.'

I did what I was told and watched the video, which was, in truth, no more than a post about five minutes long and showed this oke in overalls and one of those multi-tool belts round his waist, a lot like 'Super Mario,' constructing what just looked like a garden shed.

'Are you sure this is right?' I said, 'all he's doing is nailing planks of wood to each other. You can buy them at Homebase.'

'On no, you can't' said Verna, 'you've got to use those special planks, the ones called Plancks.'

'Jewson?'

'Doubt it, they've got to be a certain length, which they can't do in a builder's yard. It says how long they've got to be, read it out.'

I looked down the list of materials and read:

'Planck length: 1.616255(18) x 10 (power) 35 m: SI units.' Verna looked perplexed, 'that doesn't sound right.'

'I could try Travis Perkins.'

'No, I mean it sounds far too long. Check it again.'

I did so and saw my mistake immediately: 'Oh sorry, it's 10 (power) -35m: SI. Then that's very small. Looks like you'll be pint-size after all.'

'That should be plenty to stretch my elbows,' she said, 'hopefully a clutch of new dimensions will start to kick in around the Quantum field, provided of course we use string instead of nails.'

'Don't tell me, Ryman's won't have it.'

'Not a chance, especially the type of string we need. Symmetrical Superstring.'

'Any suggestions? Like I should google. Plancks and Superstring?'

She frowned, grimaced and brightened, all in less than 10 (power)-35 nano seconds.

'Try E-bay,' she said finally.

***

At least we were now in my territory; what I didn't know about Quantum fields would weigh less than a Higgs-Bosun. The problem was still that even if all the parts fell into our laps right now, 10 to the minus thirty-five nanosecs was a good approximation to how long this shed would stay upright if I built it. Next day Verna called: 'Is it ready yet?' she asked.

'Nothing on E-bay,' I had to report, 'not even the string.'

'That'll come with the Plancks as a job lot. Are you sure you're looking in the right place? Don't forget you need Branes as well.'

'Well, if you don't think I'm up to it, get someone else,' I said, not inconsiderably nettled by the perceived slight.

'Not brains, Branes, sweat stain, so the string can vibrate in its Quantum configuration, otherwise you'd just have a lot of distressed Zaptowaves, drifting aimlessly in space. Stick that into your E-Bay search and you're bound to come up with something. I'll come over tomorrow and we can make a start, bye.'

I guessed that if her team and mine's grasp of theory were all that were needed, we'd have the mother of all ugly black holes nailed by now. Unfortunately, that was part of the problem, as when you followed the black hole self-assembly route you had to use Superstring instead of nails. I decided to try and kill two birds with one stone and find a local builder who could not only do the job but also get the supplies in. Needless to say, it didn't work. Plumbco had trades of all descriptions and even quoted me a price for the job, but when I told them about the queer things, we wanted to assemble it from the line went quiet before they came back with a 'nolle prosequi,' jobwise, unless I procured the parts for myself.

So, I went back to E-Bay, this time incorporating the wretched brains, pardon me, branes into the search, and to my very great surprise it worked. What's more the site, whose address was encoded, agreed to have them over by mid-day. I re-connected with Plumbco who said they could come over and make a start later that afternoon, which they did, and by paying the men a generous double-time, plus a bung, they had it finished by 9.30 pm, thanks to the Acme stadium lights Verna had her assistant bring over, which had been intended for that rave she planned. That only left the Quantum particle-collider engineers to sort out the black hole, then tidy up any odd neutrinos left lying around.

I have to admit to a quantum of trepidation when next morning came around; not only was I sceptical that the unprepossessing garden shed we had built last night would withstand the trauma of those much anticipated extra dimensions held within, but I was becoming increasingly conscious of the bigger picture in which one party, namely Verna, was preparing to enter a world of which we knew next to nothing, while the little we did know alluded to forces so immense that the laws of physics and mathematics got ruined; while the other party, namely me, remained like a dummy, safely ensconced in a back garden off Fulham road. In addition, there was something oddly bizarre about making a journey which had the potential to ultimately unify all the scientific understanding so far amassed in human history, with the Quantum world, of which our true understanding was about as microscopic as the sub-particles which inhabited it, just to pick on one single bacterium, solely to obliterate it from the face of the earth, while anything else we encountered along the way would be lucky to get an entry in the footnotes. Quite the telling narrative for just another of life's little ironies!

Next day when I opened my front door to Verna, I can't say that I felt reassured. For a start she was dressed as if she was just taking the dog for a walk in the park, that is slacks, t-shirt and trainers. I don't know if I'd been expecting some sort of casual equivalent of the full-metal Chernobyl inspection kit, but I did rather suppose that some protective clothing would have been a good move, over and above the anorak she had draped across one arm, obviously grabbed from the hat stand by her front door as an afterthought just as she was leaving.

'No woolly?' I baulked.

'I'll be fine,' she said bullishly; 'plus the brolly in my bag has been tested in a wind-tunnel, just in case atmospheric conditions inside start playing up. Is that it in the garden?'

'Affirmative Cap'n,' I answered playfully, 'built according to all specs and only completed last night.' If she's un-phased, I thought to myself, why should I gnaw at the marrow.

'Right,' she said. 'Then let's make a start.'

***

'Looks the business,' said Verna confidently as we gave the hut the once-over, Plancks, Branes and Superstring presumably passing muster 'Now we need to find the way in.'

'That will be round the side on the right I think,' I said as I racked my brains trying to remember where the builders had put it. And indeed, it was, a perfectly harmless looking door, with a shiny brass knob.

'Why not put on your anorak before you start, just to be on the safe side, you can always take it off later when things settle down?'

'No,' she repeated, insouciantly, 'I'll just take it one step at a time, see how it goes. Anything else I should look out for?'

I took a deep breath, 'how long have you got?' might have been the flippant answer, however as she already had her hand on the doorknob, I kept it short and gave her a list of bullet-points.

'First, don't forget to shut the door behind you; very important that, otherwise the black hole might muscle out and consume all the rest of us, probably making a better job of it than ten thousand viruses.

'And that radiation anticipated at the event horizon, bubbling out?' I continued. 'Actually, it may be more of an intense rush, only exceeded by the velocity of all the stuff getting sucked in. Then once you enter the black hole itself, gravity gets busy squeezing matter to infinitely high densities and Spacetime itself collapses. So be sure to watch out for that. Towards the bottom of the black hole don't be tempted by any so-called 'wormholes into parallel universes,' as that whole theory has been pretty much discredited. Like Prof Hawking said, enough of the radiation will have edged its way down there so it should feel a bit spongy. With luck you won't fall all the way down to oblivion but start to bounce back up again.

'That's where the Quantum field operates, with sub-photonic quarks vanishing even before they materialise. Conceivably that's where the virus will be lurking, but it won't be easy pinning it down as we expect everything there will be discovered in a multi-dimensional configuration so your sweep would have to be incredibly thorough. However, my guess is that it may have actually out-thought the field's cosmic psyche and disguised itself as some common-or-garden photon, which is next to impossible to get a hook on. In which case you'll need to pass all the way through to the other side to have any chance of catching it.'

'I can see this taking all day,' she said, 'I had hoped to file copy back to Philomena by this evening.'

'If you can remember to count up all the new dimensions as they crop up it would be good.'

'And you remember to collect on that bet we made, so I can pay my rent backlog.'

I acknowledged her request and resumed reading out the charge sheet.

'Everything in the Quantum field is tiny. I'm thinking minus a factor of Planck masses here, including the black hole configuration itself. It should work in your favour though as the compression factor takes over as soon as you arrive, so even if you finish up the size of a neutrino you won't be conscious of it, or much else, very probably. Anyway, hopefully you'll bounce back when you get out the other side and can get back on the job.'

'Whatever,' said Verna.

'At least take a suitable precision instrument, 'I entreated.

'I'm taking my phone, that'll be enough. I'll call or SMS, unless the receptions too bad. Anything else?'

'Quantum gravity.'

'Yeah, Bernie said something about that. Like you think it will be compressing me or have me floating about like a bubble of air?'

'No, nothing like that, in fact you'll know it's about if you're still standing up. Thanks to the Superstring, the Quantum field is held together by elemental massless particles called gravitons. No one's ever seen one but that's only because the Hadron collider, wherein they're inclined to lurk, delivers about as much energy as a peashooter in a fat burger, so they disappear too fast to be identified. You could do worse than try and bring one back, help settle a few arguments; come to think of it a few bits of dark matter and dark energy wouldn't go amiss either. How are you going to catch the virus? Sorry, trap it.'

'With this,' answered Verna, brandishing a sort of mini fish net, of the type used by children to scoop up water-boatmen in a garden pond.

'That won't work, it will escape through the holes in the meshing.'

'Don't doubt the appliance of science, old bean,' she said proudly, as one prepared for all contingencies. 'Filled them all in, didn't we? Or rather my little brother did. But the clever bit is what we filled them with: special micro-sized pictures of the most frightening things we could think of.'

'Such as?'

'Loads of things: my dad getting up in the morning, a broken skeleton on a wheel from the London dungeon, a Dalek, even a miniature of Banquo's ghost, in case it's a clever sob and knows Shakespeare. Be assured, once I nab it, it will give up on the spot, then it's just a matter of transferring it to a cardboard box and asphyxiating it, just like catching butterflies on Box hill.'

'You're not meant to kill butterflies anymore,' I said, temporarily distracted by memories of a childhood idyll and that most harmless of pleasures, but quickly pulled myself together to issue an unambiguous death sentence for the V. I gave it the thumbs down, like Commodus at the Games: 'Poison it!' I said.

'All to hand,' she said confidently, 'I've got my gear on, so let's go for it.'

I handed her the list of bullet points.

'Don't lose it,' I admonished, and she folded the notepaper somewhat ostentatiously and put it in her back pocket. In view of what she faced; such harmless theatrics were in my view a veritable badge of bravery.

So, we both approached what looked to be a perfectly ordinary garden shed with a door to one side, no doubt shut extremely tight. Except of course it wasn't ordinary, but instead, provided our calculations were accurate, contained part of an unimaginable multi-dimensional universe, on a scale to make Gondwanaland seem no bigger than a doily plate.

With a total absence of ceremony, Verna opened the door and resolutely closed it shut behind her, never to emerge from it again.

« II »

Of course I had known from the minute I agreed to this that hunting down a virus would prove to be difficult and sure enough as soon as I'd closed the door there was the first setback dead ahead and all around me. I was in a Planked-up shed, hastily erected in D's back garden, laced together with Superstring, and housing, somewhere, its very own bespoke Quantum black hole. The travel plans I'd been issued instructed me to pass through this black hole to whatever wasteland remained in the Universe beyond it, where I would most assuredly find the virus 'progenitor' lurking, then bag the thing. Problem was, I had to find it first in an epiphany of dark space. (admittedly more or less what you'd expect from an empty shed) So even if there were traffic cones marking the way there, I was totally sightless and would be none the wiser.

Fortunately, I was spared complete sensory deprivation as I instantly began picking up sound vibes, jumbled-up waves of them swimming in the atmosphere. It seemed a positive development at first, as total sense deprivation is known to compromise orientation and inhibit mobility, but unluckily as soon as my ear became fine-tuned the underlying monotone divided into a sort of sonic smorgasbord, as if random sounds were competing with one another in utter tonal diffusion, now rising to strident crescendos, now diminishing into fractional semis, ultimately piling up into the most hideous soundscape to accompany me on my way. If only I'd remembered to pack the cotton wool buds!

I still couldn't see a blessed thing and found myself taking dirty great exaggerated strides using the pole of my net to poke about for imaginary obstacles. Obviously, the success of the mission depended on the string holding together, which I was told was nothing to do with its resilience and everything to do with the multiplicity of dimensions of which 'I would become conscious.' (their words, presumably because even the Super variety of the string was insufficiently developed to have a consciousness of its own.) Anyway, as I had already been briefed on the 'dimension issue,' I didn't expect the shed's internal measurements to keep to a tidy 18' x 12,' or anything refined like that, especially with a black hole in the offing, but it was still tricky making progress, with the m/o of some sort of visually challenged lepidopterist.

Nonetheless I persevered, supposing that if there was nothing to bump into it didn't really matter which way I went as I'd be sure to find the thing eventually. Also, those massively dissonant sound waves had resolved their competition issues and settled down into a rather alluring choral hum which it was actually quite hard not to join in with. I remember asking some boring bloke I met at a party once what exactly a scientific field was, (after he told me he studied them) and he came back with: 'you take a hoover at one end, (or vacuum I think he might have said) and the universal harmony at the other, and science is everything in between. Well, it sounded a bit like that.

This was all well and good, but I knew that life would get more challenging once I started getting near the hole itself, so it was no surprise when a feeling of something constricting me, like I was wearing a Victorian bodice made up of rubber bands, took hold of my upper torso and compressed my ribs as tight as a lashed steer. Then just as my lungs were about to burst the elastic seemed to start unravelling and I bounced away like ball in a squash court, only one without walls or ceiling. The hum in the atmosphere now turned into a crackle with such an edge to it that it lanced itself inside my brain, causing wild paisley patterns to gyrate in front of my eyes, only to disappear almost before I registered them, like those subliminal ads for burgers they used to run in cinemas. And it wasn't done yet; while I recovered from the temporary setback of being launched out of court and gamely prepared to strike on, I sensed the vibes become keenly sentient, probing my brain inquisitively with the thinnest of wisps that melted away before you could work out what it was, they were looking for. (or whether or not they'd found it!) From somewhere inside the rubber bands there was another sound, this time coming from my intestines, a sort of gurgling noise telling me I was missing my elevenses. From this vital piece of scientific data, I worked out that I must have been there a good hour already and all these emanations were a sign that I was getting close.

Now although I would be the first to admit that I'd not score highly on the subject of black holes if I was on Mastermind, I didn't intend sacrificing myself for humanity without a quick course in the bare essentials before the off. For this reason, I had given them the best part of an afternoon on Wikipedia, to go with the list of bullet points Daly had drawn up, which I had tucked up safely in my back pocket. I went to give it another pat for reassurance, but alas the rubber bands had other ideas, claiming my backside as part of their hegemony and lustily sending out feelers to the tops of my thighs. In the end, it didn't matter much as one advantage we had over all other black holes was that we'd constructed this one ourselves, or rather our wave-engineers had, drafting in a Quantum-particle accelerator for the purpose yesterday afternoon, hopefully giving us some sort of handle on it. Unfortunately, by then we were getting a bit pushed for time, so I just hoped that they had the chance to give it a run-through first. Besides I was sure I could remember them, or at least the important ones.

First off, I recounted: 'close the door behind you.' Well obviously, I'd done that; having not been born in a hayloft, it was virtually in my DNA. In fact, it just showed how even the boffins could get the wrong end of the stick, as they had assumed that the minute, I walked in I would be sucked into oblivion, whereas I'd had to wander the equivalent of several Hurst Parks before it started to come at me. My guess was that the elastic bands round my torso and tentacles in my brain bursting through the sonic throb meant that I must be getting near the 'event horizon.' This was another bullet point; I knew I had to be careful here as one of these very much amounted to a line drawn in the sand, the crossing of which even the most gung-ho of Caesars would have had to think twice about.

By now my eyes had become used to the dark so I stopped before going any further for a quick perusal of this so-called 'horizon.' This was where, if the well-known scientist Stephen Hawking was to be believed, some species of radiation was to be found, (probably gravitational, knowing him) and in preparation for which I had already taken the precaution of putting on one of my old Covid masks before the rubber bands had taken a hold. I stared as hard as I could but nothing, I could see fitted the bill. Perhaps it was only real black holes, the familiar ones busy digesting galaxies that it applied to and not to one's like ours which you could probably get from IKEA by now. Wikipedia said that

Hawkins said, this radiation was hugely meaningful, as if the black hole didn't leak a bit round the edges, it would just carry on getting bigger until the whole of the galaxy was swallowed up. What's more, it wouldn't stop there; the greedy thing would then start on other galaxies hanging around nearby, and before you could say beam me up Scottie it would gobble up the entire Universe. So, if I had to report back that the wretched thing couldn't manage the merest dribble the news would go down very badly, maybe prejudicing all my other findings, like hopefully the death of this froggin' virus!

Well, there certainly weren't globules of the stuff zipping about me and at first glance I couldn't see anything in the distance either, though admittedly the stars didn't appear to be out and there was zilch in the way of a moon which might have helped. I was about to give up on horizon-Hawkins radiation altogether when just out of the corner of one eye I thought I glanced something, a yellowish wisp of light, going on and off, like a dodgy torch bulb. The double take confirmed it; in fact, there were dozens of them, hundreds even, uni-dimensional by the look of it, and slithering about in between the bust-up atoms and molecules of all the disintegrating matter getting sucked in. Perhaps these particles were attracted by this ribbon of radio-active light, like circus dogs jumping through a ring of fire, or perhaps they were the cause of it and left shreds of it in their wake, like debris in a comet tail. No matter! One up to Hawkins, as his 'Hawkrad' sweeps the board after all. Just a pity he's not still around to learn the good news, he'd be chuffed to bits. Plus, a big X to all black hole supporters who should be mortified to learn that instead of getting in training to swallow us all up, they've sprung an unpluggable leak, and are busy oozing away their ill-gotten cosmic gains, like a saucer of cultures evaporating on the window ledge in a tainted lab. Serves them jolly-well right, too!

So, across the Rubicon I skipped, and was now well on my way to the next stage on the critical list, intrepid waif that I was. Luckily there was still a lot of space to be had despite the massive incursion of clutter from the stuff mentioned earlier which had been caught hovering too close to the event horizon, like those migrating wildebeest who hang around the banks of the Limpopo too long and get zapped by a croc. I had to duck when what looked like a couple of incinerated moons flew past, but apart from that I was fairly safe. No wonder there was no moonlight earlier.

But the G forces were now compressing me to minced quince, like I'd passed twice through a mangle and was still too bulky for their unintelligible taste. All remaining matter had already shrunk to the size of a plonky ball, queueing up for its turn inside the particle collider, yet still putting on weight like a strudel fetishist. As for time? Well, I had my watch on, but I knew that I was on to a loser if I expected it to tell me when cocktail hour was. Predictably the elastic bands simultaneously tightened and tried their luck slipping a bit further down my knees. Ever a glass half full sort of person, I had sort of half hoped that these somewhat grosser manifestations of collapsing Spacetime, alluded to above, might be more lightweight in our bespoke version of the hole, or even be something I might be able to control, like I could give a good yank on some handy reins attached to its core and get all these apocalyptic forces to just slow down a bit.

Sadly, there were no reins, and no other restraints immediately to hand; but at least its powers were not yet proving terminal and I could still tiptoe in tiny steps and ready myself best I could for oblivion and beyond. As far as I could work out, the next bit of disorder coming my way should be the final one anyway, namely: 'The Singularity!' Like a maelstrom with a turbulence warning, I once heard it described.

Now it's no secret about a black hole that it saves its worst until last, and so I knew not to expect a repeat of the docile event horizon experience, with its soothing wiles, and a quick shuftie about what remained of the night sky for radioactive fireflies, before a gentle skip across the divide, like Bo-Peep seeking an errant lamb on its last gambol. No, make no mistake, this was the big one, more akin to Pastor Kierkegaard's leap of faith, if I'm honest. And if he wearied with angst about the existential baggage of the soul, then I warranted brownie points for keeping my pecker up the way I did.

The way forward was starting its descent now and I sensed that vanishing point must be getting close. My trainers felt more like reinforced diving boots, with gravity tugging them onward, upward, and sideways, all at the same time. Down and down, I went, now gaining the equivalent of a three-bedroom detached townhouse for a milk-maid's yolk across my shoulders. This close, any last-minute checks seemed irrelevant, just tough it out and see what happens seemed the way to go. It could only be guesswork beyond this point; either I'd be crushed like a hedgehog on the M25, or an 'n to infinity progression' of incompatible forces would give up in irresolution and spit me out into some future or other. These days D and his team refrained from speculating what this 'future' might constitute, but wherever it was, my priority was clear: to hunt down the progenitor of this blister of a V, the genocidal pathogenius that was the cause of all the fuss in the first place. And with nowhere else to skulk and no more hosts to contaminate, I confidently anticipated a walkover once I actually confronted it. What's more the returning hero would then celebrate her 'triumph,' and after all the plaudits along the Apian Way had run their course, I would boldly fob the Senate off with all the petty details of this post black-hole future in a sort of minority report.

Years ago, it was ever popular science to imagine that here might lurk squillions of wormholes in the Spacetime-continuum, like convenient trap doors to get you out of any mess, and deliver you, like some sort of inter-stellar Thomas Cook's, (RIP) into one of an infinite number of parallel Universes. So, any time some astrophysics pointy-head got him or herself fogged by the odd equation that wouldn't work out, or radio pulse which couldn't be traced, out came a convenient warp or wobble in the fabric of Spacetime to explain it. Nowhere was this truer than with 'Big Bang,' the frankly nonsensical attempt to explain the beginning of the Universe as 'originating' from an explosion of nothing from nowhere, but which nevertheless remains the popular and prevailing view to this day. For if you can instead stack up an infinity of parallel Universes, how any one of them got started hardly matters. Same with the end of the Universe: inflate it, deflate it, or just watch the lights go out, no one need bother any more about the nothing and nowhere you're left with on the other side because you can just slip into another one close by, like they were on a rack at Primark, until that one packs up; and so on, until they're all used up, which of course they never will be. As for any intrepid time-traveller looking for adventure now that most of our own world can be detailed on Google, well, TV and cinema has long since had that base covered. What could possibly entertain us more than a parallel universe where everything is one bit the same and another bit different. No limits, no laws, and no surprise when the average ape sat in the canvas chair sets the scene so Captain Kirk can roam the cosmos just to fall in love with a Barbie-doll. So, to expect to find a parallel universe at the business end of a black hole was pretty much par for the course, had we been doing this thing pre-millennium, say. Now we know better.

As D had instructed me, once he'd finished floundering around trying to find a supplier, it's the privilege that Superstring brings to the table that allows us to make this journey, so we can pick Branes, tie up Planck lengths with string, and construct a shed with a black hole inside. It was at this point that he came clean on the dimension situation. An important consequence of our nascent Superstring mechanics, apparently, was that our dimension myopia would come to an end. Post general relativity we have of four of them, five at a push; but once we'd finally passed through the black hole then we confidently expected to experience nothing short of dimension enlightenment! So, another of the bullet points had been for me to keep a tally 'en route.' Extra duties, more like, I mumbled under my beard, but in the end, I acquiesced meekly, like the frail petal I am.

Once they got wind of what we intended to do, Paddypower, I think it was, started to give out odds on how many there were to be discovered. This was the opening show:

Just one more:	3 – 1
Two more:	5 – 2
Three:	5 – 2
Four or Five:	10 – 1
Six to ten:	25 – 1
Eleven or more:	80 – 1

D had read in some research paper or other that one Superstring jobber using a rare branch of multi-linear algebra had worked out that one-dimensional Superstring meant there would be precisely fifty-nine new dimensions just waiting for someone to drop by and classify them. So, while we were waiting for the paint to dry, we all chipped in a tenner and D went over the road to place the bet. All told (including carpenters and caterers) there were twelve of us making a total stake of £120. He actually got 100–1 on a 59 target, the layer's teller obviously thinking he knew a mug when he saw one. But the intelligence was in the public domain, no question, so we were in the clear, while something must have clicked at Paddypower Head Office, even with such a small wager as ours, which persuaded them to dig a bit deeper into the matter. However arcane a subject might be it's an axiom amongst bookmakers that if you intend to lay it then unless you know all the form lines you can get shafted. No surprise then when thirty-six hours later, just as I was about to step through the shed door, that all the above had disappeared and shortened to less than the price of a BHS share. Suddenly, up to fifty (more dimensions to be discovered) was at odds on, only widening to evens or better beyond fifty-nine. Precisely none of which mattered to us as we had taken the ante-post price. But it was the final piece of intelligence I received before I left, as a not-so-subtle reminder, again, to have my check-board ready when I got to the other side. And it was not as if they would all be milling about with labels on waiting to be sorted, like trains to be spotted; they would most probably be like those animals in habitat-friendly zoos, which just slope off as far away as possible as soon as dinner's over so that nobody can see them.

However, all this was far from my mind now as I closed in on the final phase. Suddenly the steep descent turned into a sheer drop which I was too weighed down to avoid and I 'took an arser' over the edge, as I believe is the correct scientific vernacular. 'This is the proverbial it,' I remember thinking to myself, ever resourceful in focusing my mental energies on a logical solution to the predicament I faced. It was too dark to see if the concentration of gravitational forces had narrowed the linear dimensions about me, I hadn't been aware of anything so much as a side-panel since I closed the shed door, so as usual it was my hearing which took over sensory duties, which this time proved unfortunate as something like a climactic grinding noise down below was becoming perceptibly louder by the minute. And down below, don't forget, was where I was headed!

I've never had occasion to find myself at the centre at one of those barometer-draining Atlantic depressions which regularly queue up off Ireland before passing across the north-west of our Isles to deliver twenty-four hours of non-stop lashing rain, (I was born in Entwistle, so I know what I'm talking about), but I imagine it assaults the eardrums every bit as much the grinder beneath me was doing. I was going at a hell of a lick by now, as our sponsor sat under the apple tree could no doubt attest, and so, despite the ' glass half-full' part of the thumb-nail sketch drawn earlier, I realised that I was a goner; 'at least it should be quick,' a tiny voice muscling its way through all the doomsters managed to chime in, before it, too, was ready to throw in the towel.

But boy was I glad it had chimed up, like a pitiful, final vestige of optimism, because for the first time in ever so many Spacetime minutes, something occurred to at least give me hope. Still in free-fall remember, now I could definitely feel myself beginning to slow, not so much because of the downward force letting up, rather there was now an offsetting upward force, and at a rough estimate the relative strengths of each would soon cancel themselves out and I would be held in stasis, hanging in mid-whatever passed for air down here. I took a look down below and saw immediately what, or rather who, my benefactor was. None other than Prof Hawkins had ridden up once again at the head of the cavalry, and in the nick of (Space) time. No mistaking what was happening here: thin, slithery licks of shimmering roseate light, at flux in a void without form, and with only themselves to slip in and out of, now combining, now separating, then falling away, to start again. But the power was revivifying. It was good old 'Hawkrad,' this time in its unexpurgated form! Soon it held me in suspension, while the downforce passed me by to either side.

Going back for a minute to that alarm some people had about how a black hole might gobble up the whole of the Universe; I could never work out their problem. I always felt it was far more likely to self-destruct, as mega G's squeezed matter into tinier and tinier bits of infinite density and all the clocks started to go backwards; and now I had experienced one for myself, I could confirm that we were both wrong. Another irony in some ways, as the very thing that saved its bacon was the same 'Hawkrad' which kept its ambitions in check in the first place.

At body equilibrium, I suppose you'd call it, I now instantly spun sideways into a corridor; I could tell it was a corridor as now I had light courtesy of the ultimate in gravitational radiation and I could make out walls and a ceiling, together with the ground I stood upon. Better still, the diabolical presaging tumult of the cosmic substance grinder had been replaced by our old friend the happy hum, obviously gearing up for another subliminal raid, and somehow, I didn't think burgers would be on the menu this time around.

I had two options; well, one really, as I could explore the corridor before me, or go back to the pit and the grinder: Avanti it was!

Post black hole, or so I most earnestly hoped, I'd settle for a corridor any time. There was no sense of being in a shed any more, truthfully, there never really was, from the moment I managed to close the door shut behind me. Here then looked like something closer to normal; a passage, apparently without obstacle or hindrance, stretching ahead. Except the floor was covered in what appeared to be rush matting, and rather threadbare matting at that, which rather disconcertingly began to disintegrate the more you looked at it! I opted therefore to look straight ahead in my direction of travel, rather than fall into to some enormous void sure to open up if I stared any longer at my feet. As I ventured further, the light from the earlier radiation began to fade and was replaced by minute darts, flashing at me like tracers from every direction, then passing through me and out through the corridor wall. I don't think ordinary light rays possess mass, but these certainly did not, and the fact that they lit the way tahead for me was more like a fortunate by-product.

Much more important, they were probing my psyche again. And this only confirmed what I had guessed coming out the black hole: their earlier sortie had just been a Sunday evening poke-about into the goldfish pond. 'Will-probe' might be too strong a word for it, but I guessed if my conscious mind was about to be seriously engaged, it could only mean that there was another conscious mind on the other end. Obviously, the vibe possessed a disembodied intelligence so it was a safe bet it would have a sniff round anything of interest it might hit on and would already have got the hang of dealing with any aliens who had come its way and whose charmed lives had seen them penetrate its defences, amongst whom I suppose I should count myself. Also, I was hopeful that it wasn't out to trick me, like some of those gods' old philosophers used to worry about, or worse still, do me any harm. So, I just decided to let it go its own way while I carried on exploring; after all, I'd only been out the black hole for about half an hour of GMT, so there must still be plenty more to see. There was even a chance that if I came up to expectations as far as the enquiring mind was concerned, I could take advantage of the situation and ask it if it had any idea where that pill of a virus might be hanging about. Even after this short time, the probe's 'modus operandi' was starting to generate familiar feelings of bounciness inside my head; pleasing, and soothing too, like the relief you get as a headache starts to slacken, only without the inconvenience of a headache. Better than a massage inside your head, more like a caress, so my brain waves just rippled and gently lapped the edges of my mind.

But was the object of this probe an attempt at communication? It would make sense, having learned all about me; but I was beginning to have my doubts. I tried rigging up an imaginary antenna, but it made no difference, those probing, supple, darts had now slowed to a trickle, and it looked like the light was starting to give out further up the corridor. A few light pulses biffed about but that was quite frankly pretty small beer after all that had gone before it. Still, I thought it odd, as you'd think anything capable of this sort of mind penetration could have managed a word or two of its own; I wasn't asking for a CV, just a 'hello and howzit' would have done. Then, somewhat abruptly, the corridor, which before had looked like it might stretch forever, widened; I was no longer enclosed, but found myself in open space; walls and ceiling fell away to be replaced by trees and sky and fresh air in between; no more grinders or vibes, pulses or mind probes, just a light breeze, the sun disappearing behind a cloud and a couple of crows perched on upright flagstones, anonymous etched memorials, whose valedictions had wasted away over time and now lay exposed to the brambles and nettles that thrived in the local humus and enveloped them, like creepers in a hothouse.

I knew where I was though, it was Brompton Cemetery, where some of us used to walk our dogs. Philomena went there and also Bernie. (the savant) Sometimes we just met by chance, more often though one of us would call the other and whoever got there first would sit on La Pankhurst's tomb (the Suffragette) and wait for the others to collect. Coincidently, the last time we all came together was when one of our associates called Henry, who had been obsessed since he was little boy with time travel, had our other associate, (Dalrymple) construct the app which could make it happen. This time though, none of them was there; instead, it was just a single face I'd never seen before in my life, a shade androgynous perhaps, but who, for the sake of argument, and/or until I knew any different, I took to be male, and who might just as well have been walking his dog, for all that first impressions were making. Probably because it was the least surprising thing which had happened all afternoon, I went over to get a closer look and he gave a me a perfunctory wave. He might have smiled as I approached, it was hard to tell as his features seemed stuck in their unprepossessing pose, making any speculation about his character or attitude profile next to impossible; more disquieting, when he moved his lips, wave patterns shaped the physiognomy rather than facial muscles.

'Took your time, didn't you?' He said. No introductions.

'Quite the contrary,' I replied, 'I haven't stopped once since I closed the shed door. I don't know how many black holes you've been through, but it soon puts paid to your time schedule I can tell you; to be honest I've done well to get here as soon as I did. And what about all that jive with the brain scanning. Anything to do with you?'

'I didn't mean you personally,' he said, 'I meant evolutionary life forms in general.'

'Look,' I went, 'we seem to have got off on the wrong footing, I'm Verna. Who are you?'

'You're right,' he answered, 'I apologise, I'm Max. Pleased to meet you. I see you have come with a purpose. The fishing nets?'

Something though was troubling me, after this brief burst of complaisance from Max, those wave patterns where his lips should be had the weirdest effect on his animation. It troubled me far more than his mistaking my butterfly net for a fishing net.

'Are you a hologram?'

'Let me explain,' replied Max patiently. 'First, let me say how you appear to me. You see I know where you're from and I also know that your people's understanding of elementary cosmology is so inept that you shouldn't be here at all. Nothing personal, of course.'

'We would call that a paradox.'

'That's because linguistic riddles are your best guess round here, and most of those you can't solve either. As for cosmic ones, don't get me started; like when you can't make sense of the rudiments of a black hole you decide Einstein should take a breather and use Quantum theory instead, backing the losing horse, as per usual, computing dimensions upwards instead of downwards, even though they're only hypothetical in the first place. So, when you can't work out how to reach the nearest black hole in your own galaxy, which quite honestly Buck Rogers could do with a pencil, you figure it would be a lot easier to make up your own. That means half-assed bronze age engineers fixing one up in the back of some 'Heath-Robinson' Planck shed and sending you to see what's at the other end. That's about the size of it isn't it?'

'Actually, that's not quite right. I'm here to trap a virus, and kill it, or at the very least anaesthetize it. Look.' I gave the net a shake.

'The people who sent you stumbled on a quirk of Quantum methodology which delivered a momentary window of micro- access by sub-particle constancy; that's how come you're here.'

'You might be right there,' I had to admit, 'I was told to grab the one called a graviton while I was here and then check out if Quantum gravity existed. Is that anything to do with it?'

'You're still standing up, aren't you?'

'Funny, that's what D. said.'

'Who?'

'It doesn't matter.'

'In fact, I'm not a hologram, rather, I'm a sort of distillation of the Universal grammar. In a while you shall come to see this as helpful, but for the time being it's problematic, because as far as I can tell, misunderstanding the Universe is quite inherent to your species.'

'Like what, and says who?'

'Big Bang for starters.'

'Not us, we crocked that along with space invaders.'

'Fair call,' he admitted, 'I know your probe absolves you personally from that particular chimera.'

'And D's time travel app says the Universe doesn't end at the same point it didn't begin at either,' I added for good measure. 'Like a hyperbola with a destiny, was the way he put it.'

'Well, I suppose he's half right,' Max conceded gruffly, 'but your real problem is you can't fathom the 'infinite' which lies beyond, or indeed, the nothing that precedes it. Now that really would be something!'

'If you're not a hologram, then what are you? Can I touch you? You don't move like we do, and your face looks funny. No offence.'

Max blew out his lips in exasperation, making them momentarily dart in different directions. 'I'm not a person, I'm an embodiment of something quite different. Like a logged-out download of Universal Consciousness into a single persona; so, this 'I,' in front of you, has to adjust to how you think and then think for itself using similar processes: but you're right, things are a little shaky to begin with.'

'A bit like us trying to work out what makes a bivalve tick.'

'None taken, but a worthy analogy. There, I think things have finally settled into place. Sorry about that: now, where was I?'

'Giving me grief about what a sad life form we are.'

'Well, I ask you? Who else would try to calibrate the universe by putting a telescope in a spaceship and shooting it at a radio pulse! Expecting it to show you where the finishing line was, like it would be there drawn in the sand. 'Oh Look, it's escaping! Better send another before it disappears altogether, and this time launch it from where the last one finished up.' On the shoulders of giants? Pah.'

'Well, it's got me here, hasn't it?' I answered. If I'm honest I was starting to get a bit put out being slagged off by this badly drawn boy of a cartoon cut-out.

Again, Max back-pedalled, blaming his petulance on problems of adjustment to the unfamiliarity of an ego. Obviously, these, whatever they were if they weren't people, were so far advanced that as soon as you dangled the assumption of a bit of arrogance in front of them, they grasped it with both hands, whilst at the same time claiming sanctimoniously, they were simply getting used to their new dexterity. I gave the virus mission another goes; I thought that if I went about, it more obliquely, I might have more luck.

'It was our science which designed this,' I said proudly, giving the 'fishing' net another shake, 'but if you know a better weapon, I'm happy to give it a go.' I should have guessed it wouldn't work.

'You remember those light pulses which came at you just before we met? Well actually I do admit that was all my doing; a forlorn attempt, as it turned out, in the unlikely event that you might just be able to grasp something of what the Universe really is.'

'How are a few blips of light meant to unpick the universe?' I asked, without prejudice.

Max seemed unwilling to comment on the merits of his own techniques, and far happier dissing ours, so I guessed his human persona was coming along.

'The Universe is consciousness, pure and simple,' answered Max, with a dogma made up in Ursa Major. 'Nothing like your Noddy book model, existing in 'so-called' space and time, with agendas and issues and endless puerile questions, like what's the point, and does it go on for ever, or isn't it dull with nothing to do? Instead, your Super-symmetry people expect you to come back and fill in the gaps with all the new dimensions you're meant to find, plus a couple of Quark bridges into the bargain. In this wise would you lay aside those fetters of ignorance once and for all, so those troglodyte 'earthers' you call scientists may break out of the prehistoric cave of darkness and superstition and ignite the dawn of enlightenment. Just so you know.'

'So, what is it that you're conscious of?'

Max's declamation hit a red light at this one; a few seconds later it turned to amber and stayed there, meaning, I suppose that even he didn't think much of the answer that eventually frothed out.

'That which remains after all generic consciousness has been sublimated and transcended,' he answered, cagily.

'Uh-huh.'

Still at amber, he had another go. 'Look at it this way,' he said; 'all those unanswerable questions you have, like where do I come from, why am I here, or is there a God, are rendered nonsensical by the misapprehension of your most elementary senses. You plod along, maybe rationalising them to explain why you feel as you do, or whether what you perceive pre or post-dates your axioms, then speculate grandiloquently, but as for an answer I'm afraid you're still at first base.'

'Then maybe we're misusing language or asking the wrong questions.'

'You use language to tell of experiences and share their commonality' replied Max, obliquely, 'it has little value beyond that.'

'So, what you're saying is that this Universe of your's...'

'Uh-uh, not mine.'

'Sorry, that this Universal consciousness goes beyond everything we can say in words.'

'Nearly right, though of course we can chat about everything else.'

'Could you convey it through art?'

Max hit another amber for a minute, no doubt unwilling to get his hands dirty in a slew of cultural aesthetics. When he eventually hit green, he replied, succinctly: 'You might as well try to build a Tetrapak model of a red giant. It's not just words which are inadequate, it's artifice as well.'

'Sounds fairly boring, if I'm honest; anyway, what about my virus?'

'There are no new dimensions to discover,' went Max, deciding to answer something he thought he asked himself several minutes ago, 'because there are none in the first place, just like there's no zero and no infinity, or Spacetime in between; and all the relativism which you invent in which throw up all these theories, questions and paradoxes of yours, are just so much moonshine.'

'You know what?' I said. 'I think I can live with that. But my name really will be mud if I don't deliver on the big V. And if you're so clever, how come those pulse probes didn't give me the slightest idea of what you're talking about?'

The intermittent silences between Max's answers were still halting, which gave me the chance to clock this manifestation of being, whatever it was, which I beheld. It was still the mouth which took centre stage. It just looked wrong, slithering about like that; for a start it made it impossible to lip-read whenever the audio was on the blink. (frequently) It also gave me time to think; there he was, saying how backward we all were, back in the boon-docks of West Brompton, and that we couldn't hope to understand the real 'Oooniverse,' (he had an extra big slither about that one) because it was in fact just an indivisible force of consciousness; while the sum total of what we knew, or ever could know, wouldn't get us much further than a lunar PlayStation, not even in a billion years, which, according to Mistermen features, didn't exist anyway. There was an obvious lacuna here in this bloke's fabric. I mean if this mega-conscious Universe really is the Pepsodent of the Cosmos, then how come it couldn't even design a simple probing pulse, let alone a proper mouth. Coincidentally, Max's unaccustomedly long downtime had led him to somewhat similar conclusions.

'It's been divined,' he began modestly, 'that the digitised 'I' will assume a personality compatible with one such as yourself, in place, time, and intelligence, in an endeavour to present a model of an unmediated Universe in such a way that you 'get it.' Firstly, I must apologise for the proforma 'self' that must so far have come over to you as an arrogant and haughty prig. How am I doing so far?'

'Four out of ten Max,' I answered, perhaps a shade harshly. 'You can't just screen-wipe attitude and then solicit approbation in the same breath; you have to work on an aesthetic and spend some time letting it bed down. Downloading a persona from this ineffable consciousness of yours is the right move, though you might look around for some sexier apps when you've got a minute. I don't mind helping you, if you like.'

'Very well,' he replied. (And it didn't take as long this time, a good sign, I felt.) 'You've come here looking for evidence that sub-particles are sublimated by Superstring within an abundance of new dimensions which will open the quantum window into, well you know.'

'No, I haven't,' I bleated, 'I've told you before, until I've got perforated cortices, I'm looking for the virus progenitor so I can stamp it out.'

'Oh, all right,' said Max, generously conceding that what he thought I wanted and what I said I wanted should be on a sort of par, 'how about if we go on a kind of educational junket of the place, so you can see it for yourself. Then I can answer any questions that crop up.'

'Nothing too heavy?'

'Cross my heart.'

'And the virus?'

'We'll sic it the instant we get back.'

That Max was the reformed character he made himself out to be, I was obviously going to have to take on trust; and if he was right about time not existing, then I wouldn't have to worry about getting home late. 'Right, you are Max,' I said, 'let's do this thing.'

***

'To get the ball rolling,' he began, 'why don't you choose some distant star you'd like to find out more about, that you'd like to visit, if you only could. In the Milky Way, say, or even a distant galaxy.'

'Tell you what,' I said, not wanting to come over as a spoilsport, because I could see he was trying here, and not having seen the 'Sky at night' for several of our earth years, 'I'll let you choose.'

The time lapses had been virtually eradicated by now, quite an impressive performance, I had to admit, seeing as how he had to kit himself out with a composite brain based only on 'yours truly's' in about half an hour, and he happily assumed the responsibility I had conceded to him without so much as a blip.

'What about a radio pulsar?'

'You mean like Radio City?'

'Not exactly, but lots of them have been discovered since Luxembourg went off the air. No? Then what about a galaxy cluster? You would be guaranteed to find squillions of planets more like yours than yours is. Or even something psychedelic, like a supernova?'

'What's the farthest star ever discovered?' I asked, just to think of something.

'That would be Icarus,' Max replied faithfully (and if I didn't know better, I would swear to it that he swelled a Planck-length in pride at his erudition.) 'Want to go there?'

'Sounds fair.'

'Come on then, then I can explain a few things on the way. Follow me.'

So, I did, not that I could see there was anywhere to go, for either him or me, our conversation having been confined entirely within an enclosed empty space which had somehow replaced Brompton Cemetery sometime after Max pitched up. Now this backdrop simply fell away, and I found myself walking across a wide concourse of asphalt, following Max as instructed, towards a gangway leaning against a snazzy looking space-hopper, a bit like a groundhog on stilts. Inside, it was kitted out like a tastefully appointed high-end comfy-zone: soft chairs dotted about, coffee table, cups, percolator, icebox, Persian rugs spread languidly on parquet floor, plasma screen on one wall, the other three fitted with reflection-proof, frictionless, laminate windows; full-on visuals to the night sky. Bit better the EasyJet then.

Max went straight to the computer on a desk built into an alcove in the far corner.

'Won't be a minute,' he said, 'help yourself to coffee if you want; though there's booze in the fridge if you prefer.'

'Can I get you anything?'

'A beer would be good. Thanks.'

I opened the icebox and mixed myself a rum and Kokta, a rather ersatz Serbian version of coke, and grabbed a lager for Max, some middle of the road Belgian brand with a screw top. By the time I'd taken them back to the table Max had come to join me.

'Cheers,' said Max. 'Is it all right if I call you Verna?'

'All the hiccups ironed out I see. Don't get to like it so much you can't bear to go home.'

Max smiled confidently, physiognomy and personality obviously satisfactorily assimilated.

'It's the least I could do to make up for the way I sounded off earlier. This way I get the chance to show you some way off bit of sky of your own, which I promise will definitely put you one up if ever you come across any of those Nobel okes. And while I think on, don't get stressed about any of that, 'can this be real' business. I've a mother of a handle on that one, trust me.'

With that there was an immense rumble from somewhere outside the ship, as great sheets of electronic flame momentarily flashed across all three windows before all sense of the ground was lost in an enormous upward thrust.

'Just to elucidate,' went Max, 'we took a short-cut back and blasted off straight through your planet's gravity, out of its solar system, beyond the Milky Way, heading for the requisite galaxy; that's what I was doing over at the computer, setting the co-ordinates. It's exactly the same as when you fire a rocket into space from earth only we were out of your sun's orbit before I started speaking. Obviously, space travel for you hasn't get much further than the nearest planet because of the immensity of the distances you perceive. We can be less circumscribed, so we'll be sure to arrive at Icarus once we've relaxed a bit, freshened up and had a bite to eat. Now tell me a bit about yourself.'

I wondered how far Max's acquired self, evidently now fully acclimatised to the outward social graces, had fared in downloading enough of an empathetic persona just to chat away over a pint and packet of Roncheros. Only one way to find out.

'I came to London from the north,' I began, 'and went to Hortensea road Art college, where I met D. He'd already done technology at some college off Old Gloucester Street, and that was enough to get him into TV. He knew Philomena and I did some work for her. It's all about who you know these days. Then we all came together on this project, sort of, though as you can see, I was the one left with the parcel in my lap when the music stopped. To be honest I've had to look most of it up on the internet, and still ended up telling D what to do, so he's not so clever as he sometimes thinks he is.'

'What about family?'

'Parents are still alive. I stayed with them until I went to Art College, then about six of us moved into a studio in Edith Grove, near the football; it was great though, same road as the Stones lived in. Not when we were there, earlier. Lots earlier.'

I paused for a moment and looked at him. He was asking the kind of thing people do when they're meeting a date for the first time, and if the answering party had an average set social skill, they would be sure to ask the asking party the same. Except with Max, it was different. I could not turn the conversation round back to him, as we both knew that he was an invention, even though the persona was now, after those few teething troubles, right on the money. Still, as we'd been getting on so well, I decided to take it back to where we had left off. That bite to eat he'd mentioned earlier would be a good start, I thought, but he beat me to it.

'Ready for dinner?' He said, uncomplicatedly.

'I'll say.'

'Any preferences?'

'Not really, as long as it's not MacDonald's.'

'Though you'd not be averse to a well-cooked burger, with garnish and trimmings? Cheese and onion too?'

'Now you're talking.' I replied. I was impressed, Max correctly supposed that an antipathy to that epitome of industrial scale food death meant a more than average liking for the real thing: 'I could murder a good burger.'

'Wine? Or beer, soft drink? Water, obviously.'

'If you're having wine Max, I don't mind sharing. But I've got no idea. You choose.'

'Very well,' said Max, 'and I'll join you with the burger.'

It went a bit quiet after that, and our attention returned to the view outside. 'Can I ask how far it is this to place we're going to?' I spoke.

'Of course, you can. I was just alluding earlier to the mismatch between the true universe and that nursery-level patchwork quilt that science has vouchsafed to your astronomers. It's about twenty billion light years there and back, give or take. To be fair one of your own desert telescopes went and pouched it a year or two back. We should be there shortly after we've eaten, but we can always park up if you're tired and need some sleep. See how you feel.'

'Must be going at quite a lick then.' I spoke. 'And I can't even tell we're moving; just like one of those bullet trains.'

It was true; not surprisingly, outside was just a mass of stars. They didn't appear to be moving yet when you glanced back at them in between snippets of conversation they looked completely different from before. At least I think they did. To tell you the truth, if someone had come and rolled up a black screen with white dots on it where the window was, I wouldn't have known any different.

'There's no way we could send a rocket this fast if I was back on earth,' is there?' Even I knew that much, if only from Thunderbirds. 'Are you going to tell me how it's done? Like there's no warp drive hidden behind a curtain or anything. You did say none of this was pretend, remember; we're really doing this trip?'

'Indubitably,' replied Max. 'Ah, I see the food's arrived.'

And indeed, there it was all laid out; side plates, relish trays, garnish, cruet, and the burgers giving out great beefy smells. Was Max's tummy rumbling as much as mine? I wondered as we sat up at table and devoured the thing pretty much without ceremony; though second thoughts that's an injustice to Max, who made a point of opening the wine and pouring our glasses out before he started. 'Cotes de Rhone,' he said. I was none the wiser. It was certainly better than house red. The best thing though was that there was no smart-ass wine talk from Max, we both just necked the stuff.

I let him finish the bottle, (more like the dregs if I'm honest) and we just had flan and coffee for afters, courtesy of Max, from fridge and percolator respectively.

'You just 'do' the food do you,' I said, 'I mean it's just another part of this whole happening thing is it, no waiters or kitchens, like there's no pilots or anything. Presumably the washing-up will all disappear the same way, and our interest moves on to other things.'

'Well, you know how it is,' said Max, almost apologetically.

Nearly half a bottle of wine and a slug of rum on an empty stomach gave me to wondering how Max might come over if he felt like getting his rocks off. Was his 'grab some rest if you're tired pitch' from earlier, a not so subtle 'floater?' I was beginning to rather fancy the idea. God, you come all this way, why not? Join The 20 billion light year high club! How cool was that?'

Just then there was a ping over by the window, like a cosmic email had just arrived.

'Ah, we're here,' said Max. 'I vote we take a look outside and poke about a bit, so as to get a feel for the place. We needn't stay very long, and you can crash out on the ride home, which will probably take a little longer anyway.'

'Remind me,' I said, 'we've come to that farthest star, Icarus. Are you saying we go outside and wander around a star?'

'No, nothing like that, we just took the line of best fit until we found a planet like yours. Breathable atmosphere obviously, technologically about the same, though they're further ahead in space exploration, so alien arrivals like ourselves won't be a problem. One difference though, the inhabitants are only about three feet high, and their skin is green.'

'Not little green men?' I croaked incredulously, 'You've got to be kidding me.'

'Well, you have to get used to it I'm afraid,' he replied pragmatically, 'after all it's not as if we're going to settle here.'

'All right,' I said. 'Let's do it, though I can tell you for nothing that when I'm back home, selling people Universal consciousness will be a breeze compared to little green men.'

Max opened the hatch and released the gangway. It led down to a wide-open space, all tarmacked over and with the usual ancillary vehicles buzzing about and surrounded by terminal buildings. I spotted my first little green man, dressed in white overalls making a beeline for our ship, brandishing a handful of papers.

'That's fine,' said Max, accepting the dox, 'we can fill them in on our way out of here. Do you by any chance have the keys to our vehicle we've arranged for?'

The response was so strange, I had to look away for fear of guffawing. I think it started with a smile, as a remarkable set of metallic-turquoise teeth, like tiny steel rods appeared, instantly followed by a single squeak and then a sort of elongated baritone, as a small green hand reached into its overall pockets to produce a set of security bleepers in lieu. Max seemed to know intuitively where it was parked.

'I thought we would take the scenic route,' said Max, opening the passenger door for me before stepping round the other side and settling into the driver's seat, 'at least we'll get something of an idea of the place's interior geography before getting streetwise. Anyway, see one town, you've seen them all.'

The contraption we were in headed out of the airport without any officialdom showing an interest and we soon sped away into the distance. The land was flat ahead and open fields stretched either side of us, with little sign of habitation, just a few odd settlements which could have been farmsteads if it wasn't for the singular lack of crop, animal, or man in situ, green or otherwise. Max explained.

'In fact, these people have such a veneration for nature that they maximise the fertility of the land by distilling its essence, which then becomes their principal agricultural resource. Production itself is way out of sight and mostly below ground. You can just make out the course of the principal river in the distance. Not only does it flow through the main town, which we'll return to, but it also makes the soil incredibly rich for miles around, just like the Nile in ancient Egypt, except it's fed strategically below ground instead of having to break its banks on the surface. What do you think of the car? No wheels of course, so there's no need for roads, just a standard self-generating energy pack to power it. Look, it flies too, so I can show you what it's like way off in the far distance. You can just make out the blur of cloud on the horizon? Beyond that is just awesome.'

I once went to Snowdonia with the school, but I must admit this was even better. The peaks rose like great jagged needles out of what looked like steaming volcanic cauldrons, blasting out molten rock in great sheets of steam and flame, as if their very souls were being summoned. The entire landscape was covered with ice at the higher altitudes, and canopies of snow drifted into crevices or hung at precipitate angles across divers ridges and atop massive cliffs, the crystalline grains glinting in the sunlight, striated through a prism of green, naturally, like a great spreading counterpane.

'They're the best bits,' said Max, already banking the ship in an arc and setting a return course into the Satnav. 'Let's head back into town and grab a beer, see what you make of the locals!'

It was no surprise to discover that the city was called Greenpoint, and unlike any of the countryside we'd seen was bustling with people, namely the little green men.

'Women too,' I suppose, I said as we arrived inside the city limits and signs of civilisation such as housing began appearing, soon clustering into local neighbourhoods, then aggregating in larger and more varied blocks towards the city centre. Likewise, clustered in concentrates along the sidewalks, the little green men bustled along about their business, mostly attired in one- pieces, not unlike the tunic worn by the only one we'd met so far at the airport. On closer inspection they appeared to be androgynous, thus answering my own question in the negative.

'Not quite,' replied Max distrait, as he fixed his attention on manoeuvring through heavy traffic; 'there are two sexes apparently, and they pair off to breed in the normal way, though I can't figure it, as I can't tell one from the other. I'll Park up soon as I can, then we'll check out some of the local dive bars. They love these places, so I believe, fraternising and misbehaving; so maybe sex is a bigger thing than we imagine.'

There was no faulting the quality of Max's research. He'd promised me a practical resume of a new planet and its people in less than a day, and he'd made an impressive start.

We left the car in an empty bay, Max aspirating our good fortune under his breath as he held me by the arm and cajoled me down what looked like a fire escape.

'This place came recommended,' he announced as we reached the bottom, including, apparently, how to overcome the tiresome entry protocol on the front door, by using the cell he'd acquired from somewhere to credit the personal account of the little green man running the pit with enough pecuniary numbers to make the tiny turquoise steel rods in his face jump up and down, like bodkins in a Bengali sweatshop. Credentials cleared, we headed further down a passage and when we reached the door at the end Max opened it and peeked inside. Then he just said, 'follow me,' as our inner space was instantly transformed into a great swarming mass of little green epicenes, I suppose we should call them, intent on moving between where they could conveniently relax with their chosen parties, and the bar from which they could obtain alcohol. Like a normal pub, in fact. Bizarrely, the scene had now been extended to include others of a similar persuasion from nearby planets, except, instead of green, they were red, orange, yellow, and every other colour of the rainbow, as well as blends in between, and all strictly demarcated within their own very separate clusters. Personally, I had an aesthetic preference for the 'battle in vain' extremity of the mnemonic, though until Max filled me in, I had no idea of what was going on here.

'Here, keeps the tab, just in case,' he said, having returned from the bar without mishap, clutching a pair of glasses filled to the brim with a glutinous green juice, which gave off a sort of muffled hum, presumably registering approval of the thick scoop of green ice cream crammed in on the top.

'It works a bit like this,' began Max, 'a person's colour is determined by the planet he or she is from, the more adjacent the colour in the spectrum, the nearer the planet. That, however, is as long as they keep to their natural pigmentation. The big deal though is that they're nearly all capable of changing colour, and do so quite regularly, almost at the drop of a hat. That is, everyone else except the little green men. All the rest can and do, and do so both as a kind of fashion posture, to flag up new tones on which they've been experimenting, and also as a sort of taunt, effecting all sorts of outrageous hues to cock a snook at any others who they want to put down, especially the little green men, who can barely squeeze the next hue along from an olive out of their skin, despite straining every nerve in their armoury.'

'If the LGM were anything like the people in our world, they'd probably put a ban on anyone entering from another planet dedicated to out-shining them.'

'It might have come to that, except there's a long-standing pact which guarantees freedom of entry from other worlds in the interest of trade. To that extent alien races such as us barely register as anything out of the ordinary, unless of course we start to change colour.'

'That's funny,' I remarked, 'because I've had the distinct impression that while the chameleons in indigo and violet have been going through their routines, the little green men have been giving us some pretty snotty looks.'

'That may well be the case,' sighed Max, as if saddened by any putative instance of ethical peccadillo in the cosmic order, 'they're a pretty conservative lot, and tend to look down on those they regard as beneath them, such as we, who can only muster a permanent monochrome. At the same time, they have a massive inferiority complex against those 'chromatic flash Harrys,' as the vernacular has it, who dedicate their lives to showing them up as 'uni-tinge.''

'You might think they'd avoid cosmopolitan places like this and stick to the own ghetto-bars in that case.'

'The last thing you need to know about the 'LGM' is this,' instructed Max. 'Their life's work is dedicated to finding a way to match the skin altering skills of their different rivals. Taxes here are colossal, all to fund massive research programmes in both the universities and the commercial sector, and bursaries are awarded to the top scientists to follow the calling. And they're happy to pay because any sort of result would immediately change their lives, from the pariahs they are now (though they'll never admit it) to potential 'Top Dogs.' Meanwhile they just stew in an odd mix of disdain for those whose meretricious posturing's are beneath contempt, and trust, that the elixir of life will be theirs as long as they are patient.

In other societies such a profile could well see them sectioned as nationally psychotic, but they're not worried as it just spurs them instead on to try their hand at the 'dark arts'. So, a whole network of espionage and subterfuge, initiated mainly by the LGM themselves, exists to infiltrate what they perceive to be the hub of other worlds' primacy in all theatres of skin-toning, principally their fashion industries as well as in-house research facilities. And naturally, as they are unable to insinuate themselves as plants abroad, so they must recruit other nationals to act as their spies. It's a fascinating narrative of skulduggery, as 'bona fide' moles take the LGM shilling and give them AI intelligence, while all manner of fake stuff passes to and fro, usually through a nexus of trained double agents, or sometimes, when the opposition get wind of what's going on, just by dangling misinformation under the noses of those spying for them, before having them arrested and punished outrageously for treason.'

'Fascinating Max, and all this time we've not even mentioned those parties on other tables which appear to be grown up rodents with exceptionally large heads.'

'Now they are another story altogether. Even though clusters of them have bedded down here for as long as anybody can remember, they have obviously followed some altogether different evolutionary path, where rodents, principally, but also some species of birds have discovered that to make further progress they need to increase the size of their brains. I suppose it's true to say that we've caught them roughly halfway along the scale, where they've got as far as evolving a larger cranium, but without yet increasing the size of their brains commensurately. Ironically, by the time they have, in a few milliards or so, they'll realise how incongruous they look and will have to spend a few more milliards concentrating on how to miniaturise their new intelligence into a more aesthetically pleasing head. By the way, how's your drink doing?'

'Fine. I remember something similar when I was growing up, called Cresta green drink; though this is slightly more ersatz.'

'Have you tried standing up?'

Even as he said it, I could feel a lightness about myself, as though helium had been transfused into my cerebral cortex.

'One's definitely enough,' said Max 'Now how about we grab some culture before we leave?'

'What's on offer?'

'Oh, you know, the usual, galleries, theatres, museums. Any preferences?'

'So, what do they find to put in a museum. I mean, how far back does their world go?'

'Oh, their pre-history is fascinating,' revealed Max, 'and you won't be surprised to hear that it all connects up with the green pigmentation of these people, as does their psychology, sociology, philology and pretty much everything else. If you take your species on earth and its evolution from the oceans to homo sapiens, and the spectrum of other creatures now prevalent, it's not surprising that what your geologists and palaeontologists dig up out the ground invariably gives testament to the great diversity of your origins. And as you claim, often figuratively, it's in your DNA; it feeds into your consciousness. There's even diversity within your own species, usually along racial lines, sometimes the source of dispute and disagreement, prejudice and war, it has to be said; in other wise, more generously you might say, it's more liberating, making you more open-minded and receptive to new ideas. Now the

LGM have nothing like that; as far back as they can go, as revealed by the artefacts they find, their world has always been inhabited by little green men, occupying the principal evolutionary spine.'

'What about those overgrown rats we saw down the pub?'

'Like I say, they derive from an exceptionally different evolutionary path, at least as far as they can tell from fossils found in the rocks. There's no evidence of any marine life here either, which have caused some to speculate that in some earlier epoch, they might have infiltrated from way off the planetary map altogether.'

'Or maybe they were indigenous and the LGM were the ones who landed from the stars.'

'I believe that would be construed as close to blasphemy,' said Max, with a twinkle in his eye. 'You can probably guess by now that ancestry plays a seminal part in their world. It all ties in with the rest of their traditions and their deeply conservative nature, feeding into that perennial obsession: Whence arose 'Ecce 'little green' Homo?' Where was I?'

'Digging up bones.'

'That's it,' cried Max, 'not just bones, but all manner of artefacts, tools, utensils, decorative art, scraps of attire have been unearthed, but nothing that could possibly shed a light on the evolution of their ancestors' skin colour. Fragments of elegant mirrors, without a beholder.'

"Who is the greenest of us all?"

Even the Max I shared a burger with might have struggled with that one; this one got the allusion, I think.

'And 'who's been sleeping in my bed?" He re-joined, 'answer came there none!'

'What are about paintings?' I said, 'our ancestors left art works in caves, mostly of the animals they hunted.'

'Exactly: so, you can imagine the euphoria when cave art was first discovered here many years ago,' Max answered. 'Judging by what they found, their history appears to reject the narrative of cave-men versus hairy mammoths; the paintings discovered here have been almost totally abstract, which obviously engendered a debate in itself: was this merely the primitive art of an ignorant people, or did it transcend the figurative form and pre-ordain expressionism? And if so, how was such creativity visited on the rest of society? In truth most people didn't give a hang. They had to know one thing: What colours were revealed?'

'I suppose green is too obvious.'

'One of the difficulties of course has been to interpret these works where basic form lines were invariably absent in the first place; but that's been as nothing compared with the loss of colour over the millennia. All that has remained are the barest wisps, so etiolated, that they could only be discerned by a spectroscope; and to the profound disappointment of all, the only colours visible were yellow and blue. Later however, this perception changed radically, and suddenly a frisson of optimism took over as further tests showed them always adjacent with a gap between.'

'York Gave Battle!'

'Quite right,' he chortled, 'there was green in between them, which for some reason must have faded away over the ages. Not only was the green inheritance saved, but cheekily advanced as an explanation of how that colour alone naturally came to dominate in the years following the now validated little green cavemen, as a synthesis of the other two colours.'

'More likely they would have been little blue and yellow striped cavemen, with a green sash.' I remarked. Max's smile was reassuringly inscrutable.

'What about lore and scrolls?' I asked, cranking up what I remembered from scripture. 'Didn't someone dig up bits of Bible in the Dead Sea, or on the beach, probably.'

'We're getting ahead of ourselves here,' said Max. 'As things stood, they still had no notion of how far in the past their language went; their diggers had always been desperate to find a voice giving verse to ancient society, but to no avail. Think what that would reveal about the burning question; be it some casual quotidian observation, or something deeper, portending to a credo or philosophy.

'That is, until they discovered 'The Chaste Stone,' which is on display at the museum, to which we are now headed.'

**

Thankfully the lightness in my head from the drink barely had the gestation of a fairy soap bubble as we arrived at the museum, and I took in the edifice ahead. The V&A it was not; all that distinguished it from the lego-esque, prefabricated block 'architecture' of the rest of the City, was an un-crenelated outer crossbeam of granite, which had caused the upper storey to sag in the middle. Trusting that it would hold for at least the rest of the afternoon, Max parked outside, and we legged it up the front steps. I suspected by now that Max was somehow able to call up a parking space to order as traffic had been heavy ever since we entered the city and this time, I caught him punching into some app on his cell.

Inside, the Museum was equally unremarkable, with LG schoolkids in little white tunics almost bowling us over in their rush for the door, having just been given permission to skip off half an hour early. From the featureless, skylit, lobby ancient treasures and artefacts in glass cabinets were on display in wide open-planned rooms to either side of four corridors, set at ninety degrees to the entrance.

'This way,' said Max, loping along one of the passages. All the rooms we passed were empty by now and with the student diaspora complete I was anticipating the ten-minute round up and eviction bell at any moment. Further along however Max opened the door to a darkened room in which a melee of LGM were busy forming themselves into a queue. It was still the usual suspects, green epicenes in white tunics, but now there was a perceptible hush, a sense of veneration almost, as a great class case in the centre of the room revealed itself, housing a three-foot-high stone slab. We joined the queue filing past. 'This is it,' whispered Max respectfully, "The Chaste Stone.' They regard it as nothing short of their destiny!'

But it was just a rectangular grey block, adorned by nothing more interesting than a rash of tiny indentations. Neither did it look too sure of itself, as if somehow it felt unworthy of all this reverence being heaped upon it and would much rather slink off into a corner.

'Pretty boring looking, if I'm honest,' I whispered back, for obvious reasons.

'Crushingly,' admitted Max, 'but see the monitor next to it? We'll be there in a sec.'

What he meant was the image displayed on a screen which showed a similar slab, somewhat smaller in stature, made up of a patchwork of different shades of green, tiny, but differentiated, and allegedly omitting not a single shade of green from the entire gamut of the 'primary,' which of course, green is to the LGM.

Max provided me a commentary under his breath: 'When it was first discovered, it was called 'The Shadow Stone,' as it obviously conveyed nothing of interest that was visible, but nevertheless it had a vague sense of menace and foreboding about it. However, by then, spectroscope technology had moved on way ahead of the days of the cave paintings, and lab investigations revealed the green changeling hidden within, which is what is showing on the monitor. But it took the intercession of a rune reader to reveal its true import; for all these myriad shades were the equivalent of symbols, effectively an alphabet, of considerable substance. Then at the very bottom were four or five lines of text, in which the symbols were put to use to convey its meaning. This was the ancient source of the same language which they still speak today.'

'Like the Rosetta stone?'

'Just so; and more. The Rosetta stone comprised hieroglyphs and was soon also discovered to be phonetic. So, it could be both read and spoken. However, unlike the earlier cuneiform, the actual text of it was ass-achingly boring, like a tally of sales tax payments or something, whereas the message contained here was deep and meaningful, and led to its renaming from 'Shadow to Chaste,' like from something rather unpleasant and impending to, well it has to be said, 'Apocalyptic.''

'Actually, you mixed them up Max,' I corrected, 'the text of the Rosetta stone gave up a seminal political insight into late Egyptian society.'

'Whatever,' went Max, distrait. 'Want to know what the 'Chaste stone said?'

'As if you're not going to tell me.'

'Five lines of a simple but telling poem. Here goes,' said Max:

'There were once five seasons:

Winter was white with wilting cold.

Spring, blue with unrequited exuberance.

Summer was fiery red with wrath and ruination.

Autumn berries, black with blame and indulgence.

And the fifth season was called Faith, and it was Green with generosity and giving. This is bequeathed to you.'

'The only bit missing is: 'By the grace of God.''

'It's their Holy Grail made manifest,' said Max with a flourish, taking his cue from the communal solemnity. 'Spirituality any place can do without 'God,' in so many words. Their society had discovered its very soul.'

'Green's their religion and their despair,' I added.

**

'What say we round off with a movie?' he said, as we followed the line round to the exit, several of our number having to stand to one side to recover their bearings, having been overcome by the emotion of the occasion.

'Have we time?' I stopped myself asking; I tried to be more specific.

'Whatever,' I replied.

'I did think of visiting one of the multi-coloured planets for a change, but all their cinema is total rubbish; all spectral special effects and about as much depth as a shrunken wadi; whereas the LGM go in for real 'Art House' stuff, like thoughtfully constructed psychological dramas, with camera angles wide as a Greek Ponzi, and low-tech projectors whirring between takes. There's one showing now at the Esoldo. Shall we, do it?'

So, we quit the museum and drove not very far to 'the Esoldo,' a stand-alone building in a pedestrianised precinct downtown, and like everywhere else so far in this City, possessing totally zero architectural flourish. Even the anteroom where they sold the tickets took its utter anonymity from the museum. But Max was right, whatever it was showing seemed popular, judging by the numbers we'd queued behind when buying tickets. We passed inside and took our seats.

By complete contrast, the auditorium had real character; more than a touch of 'art-deco,' with plenty of stucco plaster cornices, honed down just enough not to antagonise the bowed corners. The colour scheme was tasteful too, the darker hues contrasting with the looming brightness of the screen. Green, naturally.

'What's it called?' I asked as the lights went down.

'Cyclops,' answered Max, and in deference to the audience, who had been quiet as mice once they'd sat down, we refrained from any further conversation until the film ended.

The 'mis-en-scene,' if that's the correct term, was a kitchen in a battered old rural cottage at some indeterminate period in the past, with only the most basic facilities. Two little green men sat opposite each other across a table and conversed in fits and starts, alternately gazing meaningfully into the distance as the other party spoke and appearing distressed all the while. About quarter of an hour in, thanks to the sur-titles Max had obviously fixed up, I realised that this was in fact a love story between a man and a woman, and though their love for one another was a given, their relationship had been compromised by their different backgrounds: he, from a poor family of free spirits, radical and forever questioning; things like the relevance of tradition, the tenets of religion, and indeed the whole conservative 'greenness' of their society. She on the other hand came from a rural middle-class community, whose values were set in stone, literally, and quite out of kilter with the liberal views of the other. (At this stage, I still hadn't worked out which one was the man, and which the woman.)

Basically, their love triumphs, despite all these fundamental mores which divide them, and after fondly embracing and giving testament to their belief in love above all else, they exit the house and make tracks for the open country, where they can be free and uninhibited, professing their oneness with the natural order, as well as each other. Cue languid wide-angled shots into the far distance, accompanying some frankly cheesy dialogue, as the camera pans the wider horizons. But an angry sky and gathering storm clouds begin to threaten their new idyll. The wind picks up and the lovers clasp each other in the teeth of a now gale- force wind, while the camera follows the angry watercourse as it thunders down from the rocks above, now eroding the underside of a disintegrating spur at the apex of its bend, now rampaging and crashing over rapids. The sound of running water rises throughout this scene as the elements come to dominate.

Then the soundtrack pauses abruptly; we see a second LGW scampering down from the top of the hill to join the two lovers. This, it transpires, is the best fried of the first LGW; she learns of the love these two have for each other and declares her great joy for her friend, but warns her, (as if she didn't know!) of the hostility she faces in their community on account of the LGM's revolutionary views and the danger he poses to established values.

However, this second LGW turns out to be false; both to her friend, and by her intentions. In fact, she's known all the time of their love, and is madly jealous, especially as she and the LGM had been lovers in the past, which had ended in great recrimination, mainly at her behest. She sneaks on her ex-lover, and while the LGM takes a step back, torn between guilt and remorse, LGW2 attempts to comfort and restrain her friend, who is on the point of re-asserting that only love has meaning, and she will stand by her man whatever. But worse is to come, LGW2 has been doubly duplicitous and alerted the authorities of the whereabouts of the LGM and the threat he represents. Next we hear police sirens from far off and the LGM fleeing in panic; and as LGW2 struggles to stop her friend running after him, we see him exposed, running across open ground, while a marksman steps out from a police car, carefully aims his rifle, and shoots the LGW in the back, all crafted in multi-angle slow motion, and unsparing of the founts of blood and viscera consequent on the penetration of a couple of dum-dums. The camera slowly, and I mean slowly, traces its way across the steppe to the horizon, where the storm has now resumed to full strength. The light fades and the film ends.

'Not bad,' said Max, blinking as the lights came on, 'though somewhat derivative, wouldn't you say?'

I knew what he meant; on the other hand, I for one still had much to understand about a people who venerated a sub-primary colour, not to mention the culture and its facets which had grown out of it.

'The bleakness of the metaphor has a certain ingenuity, for me,' I replied, just to spike his guns, somewhat.

'Still, let's meet the Director, see what he has to say for himself.'

I assumed he was pulling my leg and instantly reproached myself for not knowing better. By now Max could bring to bear just about anything that could be thought; not altogether surprising I suppose, considering he had the sum of Universal consciousness in his corner. We left the auditorium and entered a lounge, a little way off. No one else was present but there were four armchairs in the room and coffee on offer from a sidebar. Max did the honours and brought the coffees over.

'He's called Lea, by the way,' said Max distrait.

'Lea what?'

'Just Lea; they're all called Lea, with a suffix to avoid confusion. It's held on a communal data base for whenever it's needed.'

An LGM in a white tunic entered the room and bowed. Now I came to think about it there was something slightly oriental about them, despite their pigmentation, obviously. I decided it must be the outfit, and its association with the grappling arts. Max got the log rolling instantly.

'You have been described as a practitioner of minimalism. Is this a label you would recognise yourself? I'm thinking especially of the pared-down cast and the weighty matters which invariably dominate their lives?'

'Name tags are irrelevant,' answered Lea. 'The issues I bring to the table are well known and I use the actors I trust. It's for the audience to judge if I have been successful.'

Max moved on. To be honest, I thought his questions almost seemed intellectual just for the sake of it, like he was working for 'Time Out,' or 'The Guardian.' I guessed it was more the fully evolved digitised Max persona coming through here, rather than the 'Universal consciousness' having a shot at 'Pseuds Corner.' While Lea's answers were of the 'Art is truth,' variety; 'I, the 'humble' protagonist.'

'Aren't the fundamental questions you ask with so much expression in danger of becoming somewhat reductive when the consequences are only examined through the prism of the micro unit, be it a pair of lovers, family, village, or whatever? Surely a wider dissemination would have greater force.'

'I can only refer you back to my previous answer. The soul of our people exists in the village, where it still resides today. From another angle, it's the medium where I can lay the most intensity into the drama. The art which I endeavour is forged in this place.'

'To some it might appear paradoxical that you rarely make a psychological sortie into the mind of the individual per se, that is his inner self, or consciousness. Your films are more about how people are caught up in the polemic. Might you consider future development there, in regard to say, man's sense of destiny, or his search for commitment; perhaps even his redemption?'

'I believe that is already present in my work,' answered Lea, laconically.

'I understand your new picture is a thriller, set in the murky world of espionage; would you like to tell us a bit about it, eliding over any spoilers, obviously'.

'I can't say too much at this stage,' said Lea cagily, 'but as is my custom I am more interested in the individuals who find themselves drawn in, and the compromises they must make, more than the excitement of the chase. Mission Impossible it is not.'

'But presumably your audience likes to be entertained?'

'And so, they will be by thought provoking drama and action contained within those parameters, rather than vice-versa.'

'I believe some of this film was shot 'off world,' with locals drafted in for the crowd scenes and a number of their actors joining the cast. Did this cause any problems? I'm thinking here, the perennial tension that exists between worlds as they aim to procure each other's colour codes. With the Green planet chief culprit.'

'"Verite-Liberte,' from Chroma 2, co-produced the movie,' replied Lea phlegmatically.

'Finally,' said Max, 'I would like to discuss your relationship with nature in the raw. As you are well aware, geographers have repeatedly warned of the imminence of drought due to climate change. Other than the 'Hanging Lakes,' which still exist today, and are regarded as a virtual shrine, no trace of placid surface water has ever been found in the planet's history, apart from the streams and rivers fed by precipitation, and evaporating at their estuaries. Many argue that rising temperatures, attributable to men's ignorance and greed, cause precipitation to become less and rivers to dry up. You seem to use nature a lot as a metaphor for the human condition, I was wondering if climate change was also part of your agenda?'

'I principally use nature as an analogue for the fragility of man, but it's only an adjunct to the drama. I am far more concerned about the vulnerability of the individual and the political world we all inhabit. If you want my view on climate change, for what it's worth, I think it's hokum; a truism, if you will. Climate's change: it's what they do, and have done, ever since an atmosphere was bestowed on this planet, five billion years ago. For mankind to inculpate itself is a form of hubris, and a fortiori, his delusional mission to repair the damage.'

'Well thank you for your time, Maestro,' went Max cheerily, 'Verna, was there anything you wished to ask Lea?'

'Only that 'Cyclops,' is a funny name for a film when there are three principal characters,' I said, just to contribute something, "Triclops' might have been better; then maybe you could have blindfolded the cops at the end for extra dramatic effect.'

'Cyclops was chosen as a metaphor for narrow-mindedness,' grunted Lea, 'wherever it is met.'

**

'His movies do have class,' said Max on the way back, 'I'll give him that, but I'm thinking Lea's seminal breakthrough isn't his take on the 'human,' or rather, the LGM condition.'

'Going off world?' I suggested.

'Precisely,' replied Max, nodding enthusiastically, 'the real dichotomy in this society is still the colour question. Crypto-intellectuals like Lea contrast free spirits with arbitrary reactionaries in some inspiring stories, it has to be said, but the real issue remains colour change. Is it a dangerous chimera, an illusion, after the facile world of fashion, and detracting from the elemental foundation of 'green,' out of which the very soul of this civilisation was created? Or is it an attainable Holy Grail, an apotheosis, whereby they will rise to the heights of their power and fulfil their true potential?'

'Off-worlders wouldn't be too keen to bank-roll a movie like that.'

'True,' admitted Max, 'I guess any sort of consensus between them paves the way for a better future,' he added weakly.

The sun had set by now as we rode our car once more through the suburbs and out of town. If prismatic colours had been gently refracted during daylight, that certainly wasn't the case now, as the horizon darkened through deeper and deeper shades of green. Surely, they can't contrive the colour of the night sky, I thought to myself. The lights of the airstrip were visible in the distance, but Max opted once again for the scenic route to take in the 'hanging lakes,' the green planet's single claim to geographical magnificence, he said.

What they were was 'a limnological moment caught in geological time,' (Max's words, not mine) which could come crashing down at any minute and likely cause some prodigious flooding. There had been a string of them at one time, a final remnant of the disappearing surface water which the climate change zealots were always banging on about. Like them, those now remaining were shaped over millennia by the erosion of diver's softer rocks, and held in place, bed and all, by a single stratum of basalt. Once the rock under those remaining gave way, then megasplosh – disappearing the airstrip and quite possibly Greenpoint City as well. Various gantries and scaffolding present were testament to the fact that LGM engineers were on the case, doing nothing for the scenic beauty, which was otherwise quite breath-taking, as starlight seemed to dance in the lakes' lapping waters.

'Do you mind if I kiss you?' said Max, as we lay on the smooth grassy bank of the highest and most stunning of the lakes.

We'd lain there a while, Max moving on to volcanology once the lakes were done with. But it didn't take a genius to read the signs, as he edged closer, pulse rate rising, breathing more irregularly as his dreamy gaze no longer contemplated the wider horizons, but directed itself at me.

So, I'd seen it coming, and had plenty of time to manoeuvre out of the zone if I'd wanted. But I didn't. For an instant I could feel that distinctly weird effect of a mouth and lips not quite together, stemming from that earlier difficulty he had, but then it did come together, and his mouth, lips and tongue pressed gently on mine. His breath tasted like holy water laced with signal toothpaste, another sign of compromise in this part of his anatomy. His arm began to caress my right breast, then his thumb moved inside my blouse to my left nipple.

'Can we make love?' He asked simply.

When a man gets this close, and I've acquiesced, it means I'm interested, though not yet fully committed. That depends on so many things I couldn't even begin to tell, but if it happens, it will happen in a moment. In this case however, I was rather more particular.

'Max,' I said, 'just say, if we had sex, and I was instantly transported back to earth to an examination clinic, would there be any trace?'

'Does it matter?' He asked.

'I believe so,' I replied.

'I can do it either way.'

'Then go with the light touch.' I said.

***

'I was thinking,' said Max, on the journey home, 'that I laid it on a bit thick when disparaging the scientific accomplishments of your people. In retrospect I suppose I should acknowledge that they've done some good work in the Quantum field; first to get you here and second, more importantly, to begin to intuit your Superstring's attenuated wave as the fusion of zero and infinity. Maybe you could give the boffs a nudge in that direction when you get home, to offset their disappointment regarding your erroneous hunt for more dimensions.'

'I'll make a note of it,' I said peevishly, 'I'm just wondering why everybody wants to load me up with stuff other than what I'm here for.'

'Don't fret little goose,' said Max patronisingly, maybe with half an eye on an endgame when he became surplus goods, 'what sort of envoy would I be if I couldn't keep a promise.'

After that, it all went quiet for a bit; mostly all that we wanted to say seemed to have been said. What's more, the trip home took longer.

'So, are you going to tell me how we went twenty billion light years like it was a day trip?' I reminded him.

'A Universe whose consciousness can sublimate a persona can as easily manage a galaxy, it's only stuff, after all. The rest was just for effect.'

'So, we really went there, right?'

'Indubitably,' repeated Max.

'Do me a favour will you Max and write it down.'

Instead of the usual un-super string of non-sequiturs, Max picked up a scrap of paper and began scribbling.

'Light years are a measure of distance, right? From the dregs of your Superstring theory comes a trans-dimensional framework for which time and spatiality may as well not exist. All you need do you is just insert that into a compatible Quantum field, so that the correct co-ordinates will simply substitute 'y,' i.e., where you're going, for 'x,' where you are. Obviously, the equations themselves are a bit tricky, but I don't think they'll give your people any problem.'

'And underline that bit about fusing zero and infinity in the Quantum field, if you could,' I added when he was finished, 'that's all part of D's cottage industry.'

Max nodded all the while, hopefully attenuating the text to my instructions, and passed it over.

'Be sure not to lose it now!'

***

Once we had returned to the point where we started, I resumed my crusade.

'Which leaves us with a virus to catch and hopefully decimate,' I said. The net was still handy propped up against the wall where I'd left it, so I picked it up and gave it another shake, really determined this time, before we got side-tracked with any more whistle-stop visits to way-out galaxies.

'So, you expect it to be here, at the end of the black hole, beyond the singularity?' Was this to be a helpful resume, or did it presage another lecture?

'Just so, the one we built at the back of the shed.'

'Very well,' said Max, definitively, 'then this is the place to start. With all the black holes in the Milky Way and beyond unattributable, on account of your exotically wayward science, sorry, your valiant, temporarily unrequited, endeavours; creating your own has turned out to be the right move. Now let's make a start, it's got to be here somewhere.'

Encouragingly the replica Brompton Cemetery we had come back to had now trans morphed once again into an enclosed space of some sort, which could only help us locate and trap the little tinker.

'Make sure all the doors are shut Max,' I said, quickly adjusting to Max's well-meant initiative, 'the last thing we want is for it to get away now. What's outside anyway?'

'Do you really want to know?' he said sceptically.

'No, second thoughts, let's just get on with the hunt.'

So, I had the butterfly net, no longer masquerading as an extra at a goldfish pond, and we were obviously both well into the investigative zone and ready to get down to it. But then those same enclosed four walls and bare ceiling, ideal for cornering a virus, and which we'd only just got used to, suddenly fell away once again, and grew into a giant open landscape, comprising a sort of idyllic vision of the English countryside, all layered with delightful blends of colour, and birdsong, rustling breezes, and leafy bowers, complete with a cherub gurgling into a fountain, and even butterflies fluttering in their milieu. Prettier than the cemetery, agreed, but back to the drawing board as far as the virus was concerned. I was disappointed, I must say, I thought Max had a handle on it. Clearly, he didn't, and I wondered idly if it might be a corollary of the dimensions issue.

'That's more like it,' said Max, quixotically, 'now maybe we can pin the froggin' little scrote down. Got your net handy?'

'This thing is tinier than a microbe,' I went, 'how are we meant to see it out here, let alone catch it?'

'So's everything else in the Quantum field,' he replied enthusiastically, 'if anything the virus will bulge like a football. It recalls the words of one of your best-known philosophers. To paraphrase: 'The virus is the virus, and the virus has been the virus since the year dot.' There it is.'

Max pointed to a clump of pond weed, where what looked like a spawn of tadpoles were trying to extricate themselves into life. 'You're not fooling anyone may lad,' went Max decisively, 'quick, scoop it up.'

I did as I was told, wielding my net in a low arc, like it was Mayday on Primrose Hill. Up came the virus, together with more than a few strands of pond weed and a gloop of frog spawn; but it didn't matter as I quickly potted it inside the little round pill box, beloved of all butterfly catchers, promising a humane death to all lepidoptera, but lined with Ethynol, to placate D.

'Should do it,' said Max nonchalantly. 'Was there anything else?'

'Yes,' I said, 'just one more thing before I go. I mean now that you are, to all intents and purposes, fully constituted as a human being, I was thinking....' I paused and looked straight at him. It was obvious that he knew what I was going to say, but he just gave an almost faultless knowing smile and let me ask my question.

'Well, aren't you tempted to stay as you are and come back with me?'

'Oh yes,' said Max, without any hesitation, 'it would be awesome. But it could never happen because although the 'me' who just answered your question is still human, just like you, the formatting of my entire self is predicated on its reverting to its original pre-existent form.'

'You managed all right on Icarus,' I said, trying not to sound coquettish.

'That was a temporary expedient,' replied Max, not altogether convincingly, 'an extemporary bubble for an authentic liaison, and sanctioned from 'on high;' within a framework of consciousness, obviously.'

'Only now you know what makes us tick, like our emotions for one thing, and how great it is to get to know each other, even when there's only two of us. Aren't you dying to find out what it's like to be part of such a world?'

'Sounds like a proposal,' went Max, equivocally.

'Just a form of words,' I replied obliquely.

'Look at it this way,' Max replied: 'What if it had been one of the little green men had made it through the random Quantum forces that spat you out. Then he might have said the same thing to me, like how could I resist a world where all of life's challenges centred on getting the better of vulgar inter-planetary peacocks who thought it was clever to display protean polychrome skin tones like it was the grammar of life? Then I might have taken them down to planet Earth so they could take a view on how homo sapiens might react to any off-world species whose appearance differed from their own.

'The fact is that you, and the little green men and everything else, animal vegetable or mineral are just a speck in the Cosmos, each in your own bubble of existence. You people will begin, and you will end, and in between will no doubt evolve a finite number of new variants, with brains sophisticated enough to make more and more sense of it. All manner of civilisations exists far in advance of yours; one day you may work out how to reach them and vice-versa, but even if you did, and together worked out what the fundamentals of the Universe were, it wouldn't change anything. Sure, everyone could probe the Universal consciousness, just like you have, because it is interminable, which is something which you, in your bubble, could never be. And even if you did somehow extend your own levels of consciousness to the infinite, it would be illusory. No matter how many the dimensions extant in your space, or how many others you posited, they would all be within the bubble, and, ipso facto, finite.'

'I'll take that as a 'no' then Max,' I said.

'All the paperwork filed away safely,' he replied summarily, 'keep it in your back pocket with that list of yours; not that you'll be needing that anymore.'

It seemed an unsatisfactory note to end on after all we had been through together, but at least it reminded me to attend to the rest of my mission, starting with dimension spotting, which Max had got so heavy about.

'I can't go back and tell them there aren't any,' I said, 'not even the ones we started with. The bookies would clean up for a start.'

'Not at all. The zero in your maths, makes the whole exercise void, and everyone's stake will be returned. If anything, the bookies will lose out due to the extra admin costs of having laid a wholly unknown phenomenon, with no return. Tell you what, how about if I let you have a graviton to make up for it, that was part of your wish list wasn't it? And that will help you get over the dimension issue for good. Got a spare pill-box?'

I felt in my pocket and produced another.

'There,' said Max, 'and I'll mark them V and G with this crayon, just so they don't get mixed up. Then you really would be in a pickle!'

'Any chance of a gluon to go with it, I've always been rather partial to them.'

'Actually, they're a bit too runny, even out here; best keep with the graviton. Remember the anti-gravitational polarity goes into reverse on the way back, so it could come in handy. Is that it then?'

'You don't have any dark matter or dark energy knocking about, I suppose. The internet says it's meant to explain the stuff we know is there but can't find; plus, what's causing the expansion of the Universe, but you'll probably have your own ideas on that.'

'You can't find it because it's not what it is. It's just another misconception of your myopic physics. Here, give us another of those pillboxes and I'll mark it D/E – Emperor's new clothes, and all that. If anybody has an angle on it, tell them one must have consumed the other and then lost the will to live. That always goes down well in the sand pit.'

I thanked him and felt momentarily flushed, as I realised, I really had a collection of specimens worthy of a Blue Peter badge, but the feeling didn't last. I hate departures as the words always go wrong.

'Then I guess it's goodbye Max,' I said simply, 'be lucky.'

So, with a kiss rather inexpertly delivered to my cheek, partly my fault as I had just at that moment turned my head from facing him, Max looked away, so I wouldn't see him wipe a tear from his eye.

'I'll show myself out,' I said, as I watched him head back to, well, quite were, I couldn't be sure. I tried to imagine what it must be like for him to become an 'ex-being,' to experience the decomposition of a persona, even as the senses which sensed it were still in full working order. He'd tried to convince us both that downloading and remitting his 'self' here and back again just to find a suitable form to please me, would be equally seamless, but as he walked away into the cosmic sunset, I knew different, and I suspected he did too.

***

After that thing were obviously going to be an anti-climax, like the flight home after a fortnight in Barbados. Max had set the co-ordinates, (which might have come in useful first time around, had I known him) so the reverse polarity would kick in and deliver me back non-stop; leaving the poor saps on the slow train to handle all the inconvenient dis-proportionalities.

But it was still a let-down. I'd had an adventure which not even famous writers like Dan Brown or Jeffrey Archer could have dreamed up. Going back would be like a journey through an anti-galactic 'Slough of Despond.' What was I meant to do, count telegraph poles!

'There you are,' I said, as she came round the corner. 'How did you get back?'

'There's another door at the side,' replied Verna, looking a bit dishevelled.

'Did you kill the virus? Any problems along the way? Forgive me,' I stuttered, as the words came tumbling out, 'I'm just so excited to know.'

It seemed like she'd only just left; I'd been out to buy some bread and a paper and had a coffee on my way back; then Bernie had called, just to make sure Verna had set off okay, and that was it. I hadn't even read any of the paper before I had gone back in the garden to have a scout round – to pinch myself as much as anything, to convince myself that it had all really happened. It can't have been more than an hour since she went, and here she was, back again!

'I did all right. According to Max I had no right to be there at all. He said I must have stumbled through a Quantum window of sub-particle constancy, so I guess I lucked out.'

'Max?'

'He was waiting for me at the other end, expecting me even.' 'How did he do that?'

'Well obviously I thought the same to begin with; but when he explained that he was in fact a digitalised persona from the Universal consciousness, which by the way comprises the entire cosmos, it seemed a no brainer, sorry, brainer.'

'Weird.'

'It was only a temporary download for the duration of my stay; he will have gone back by now, but I'd never have managed without him.'

'Wasn't the butterfly net any good then?'

'It wasn't that it's just that without Max I wouldn't have known where to look.'

'But you did find it?'

'Yeah, it was skulking in a pond amongst the frog spawn, so I scooped it up when it wasn't looking.'

'And killed it?'

'Of course. I put it into one of those pillboxes you use to kill butterflies, like you told me. Look.'

Verna showed me the little cardboard box she meant, with a day- glow 'V' on the lid.

'Why is it humming?'

'Search me, it's probably stress vibes from the journey.'

Something wasn't right here. In normal circumstances you'd think that successfully negotiating a black hole and living to tell the tale was enough to qualify the mission a success, but I was beginning to have my doubts.

'You didn't just starve it of oxygen, did you?'

'Don't be silly, you told me to poison it, so I did.'

'With what?' I hoped she'd say Novichok, or at least Polonium.

'I can't remember. Ethynol, I think.'

'Ethynol. You used that to kill the Covid 19 virus! Ye gods! I doubt if it would put paid to an asthmatic ladybird.' I was not inconsiderably rattled, the earlier euphoria evaporating like a Martian watercourse.

'Well, it's dead, isn't it?'

'Of course, it isn't. There's probably a colony of them by now. That's why it's humming.'

'Well, apart from that I did alright. I don't know why you want to drag it up to be honest.'

'Alright? Like what?'

'Well for a start I found one of those gravitons; here.' And she showed me another pill box with the letter G on the lid this time. 'So, I didn't get them mixed up,' she explained.

'Same problem though, if we open the box it will escape.' Negativity was beginning to tilt my equilibrium, worryingly.

'Plus,' she said, producing a third pillbox from somewhere, 'Dark matter and Dark energy together, though Max said they're less of a concern as they would probably have done for each other by the time I got back. Anyway, we don't have to open the virus up, we can just kill it with a mallet, like that girl on TV, whacking those killer spidos in a banana factory.'

'Look Verna, we, or rather you, have gone and missed a trick here. The reason you travelled through deep space nine was to isolate its last refuge and destroy it. You did right to catch it in your net, but wrong not to kill it there and then. Bringing it back alive was the worst thing you could have done. Now it's just free to start all over again.'

'Well, I'm not going back and that's flat.'

'Surely this Max character, if he was so wired into 'Universal consciousness,' could have told you what to do?'

'He spent most of his time dissing us over our sad astrophysics. I kept telling him I was there to catch a bug, but he just went on about how we were all not much better than flat-earthers.'

'Well, we knew enough to build a black hole, and get you to the other side.'

'Actually, he did say our Quantum methodology wasn't all bad, say a C grade, but he trashed most everything else.'

'So apart from finding the virus in a pond and seeing you off with it in a cardboard box, what else did Max accomplish of such Universal moment? Was he even real?'

'I did have trouble with that, I must admit; when we first met the lower part of his face was still slotting into place, like the nanosec gap when some algorithms begin crunching megabytes of data. I thought he might be a hologram of some sort, but he just said that the co-ordination of the senses into a persona couldn't be instantaneous.'

'You mean that it took time.'

'Suppose so; ironic when you think about it, as he had an extra mega-dis about time; though to be fair it can't be easy joining up a persona with its cerebral cortex, straight out the box, so to speak. But he did say he was every bit as real as our trip to Icarus was. Quite ambiguous really, not that it occurred to me at the time.'

'Icarus?'

'It was Max's idea. After his systems had finally all joined up, he calmed down and asked me where I wanted to go; when I couldn't think of anywhere, he suggested Icarus.'

'Take long?'

'I was thinking about that too; I never slept at all the whole time since I left here; like I started in the shed this morning and now, I don't know to be honest, my watch stopped ages ago.'

'You've been less than an hour,' I assured her.'

'Then Icarus must have been an episode inside that time frame. Apart from a big boom at take-off, it was just like an ordinary flight; we had a few drinks, something to eat, gazed out the window at a few stars and next thing I knew we were there. Max never said much about how much time it took, obviously.'

'Did you get off?'

'Pardon me?'

'Did you leave the plane, or rocket, or whatever it was, to explore?'

'Oh yes. I think he said Icarus was part of a star cluster, and apart from being a long way off there were umpteen planets in its heliosphere, so we landed on one that was most similar to earth. We flew about a bit in a sort of convertible hire car and then went into town for cocktails. The main difference was that the people who lived there were small and green.'

'Little green men? You've got to be kidding me.'

'Do you know that's just what I said. What's more there were also aliens there who could change colour at will, leaving the little green men seething with jealousy because their pigmentation was stuck on green.'

'Leaves you awestruck at how societies of the future have advanced beyond our own.'

'Not so much,' replied Verna, for once oblivious to the sarcasm.

'So, Max takes you for a ten billion light year jaunt across the universe but still can't help you biff the virus?'

'Twenty billion there and back actually, and I told you he wasn't particularly interested, he just regarded it as a side-show; the only reason he agreed to help me was because I went on about it. But what he did do was let us in on how we could also manage inter-galactic space travel.'

'What, like Icarus in an afternoon?'

'Like I did with Max, why not? He offered to explain it all to me, but I told him to write it down instead. That was when he got round to admitting that we had, after all, made some progress in Quantum field ordination. He was more emollient by then and offered to fill in the missing gaps so that the rest of our science and cosmology could catch up. Like our multi- dimensional expectations were a bit off. So, according to Max, the only one which might qualify would be 'Planck length,' but we'd be better off forgetting about them altogether. He wrote that down as well.'

'That's our stake money blitzed.'

'It isn't Max said the bet was void and stakes would be returned.'

'Got all bases covered hasn't he, this 'Max' character,' I huffed, though I had to admit that these discoveries which could quite revolutionise the future of mankind did make me feel some contrition for reproving her so remorselessly. Still needs must, the 'res' of the matter remained to be sorted and I clung on to the hope that having been to the other side of the universe and back and enjoyed the company of, 'inter alia,' little green men, there must be an answer somewhere to the virus conundrum. Like it was probably right under our noses while we ignoble men peeped meaningfully about distant horizons, searching for supernovae. Maybe it was somewhere in these exegeses of Max's on our supposed misguided science and plodding efforts to map our own solar system. Or if the little green men lived on a planet similar to earth, perhaps they also underwent virus pandemics.

'Show me what he wrote.'

Verna pulled a couple of pieces of paper out of her back pocket and handed them over to me.

'Written by a pixel amalgam from a non-dimensional Universe,' I thought to myself, 'should be easy enough.' Unsurprisingly, they were entirely in mathematical notation; but at least the algebra looked familiar, so somebody should be able to decipher it. I could recognise some basic premises concerning general relativity, and enough of the Quantum formulae to give me precisely zero insight into whatever the key was to be sashaying across light years in an afternoon, that Max's text purported to be delivering. Furthermore, one depressing conclusion which was soon apparent was that there was nothing about Covid 19, or any other virus come to that. Despite the revolution in science which these scraps of paper would no doubt prove to be, for us, it looked like our scheme to obliterate the virus had been a failure.

'Was there nothing else, perhaps a clue from the planet of little green men? Anything else Max said or wrote?'

Verna emptied both pockets, front and back; another bit of paper fell on the floor.

'What's that?'

She picked it up and unfolded it. 'Oh, I remember, it was the bar tab from the cocktail lounge we went to.'

'Shuft.'

Verna passed it over and I studied its content Did I expect it to read:

'Two green drink sundaes...@...15. IDV?' (Icaran drinking vouchers)

Well, it didn't, and if this was a bar bill then I was Schrödinger's cat! And if these were numbers, then they belonged to no system I knew; nor were they symbols I recognised if they were script. It was sticking my neck out, but there was something about it which was did appear familiar: it was in code.

'Why on earth did he give you the bar bill?' I suppose I could have framed the question more carefully.

'Dunno, I didn't even know I had it.'

'It could be important Vee; I think it's an encoded message.'

'What, from the little green men?'

'Maybe, or maybe from Max himself. It might be the reason he gave it to you.'

'Why?'

'Who knows. Perhaps he meant you to bring it back with you. Anyway, we won't know for sure until we've decoded it.'

'Good luck.'

'It's not that simple. The symbols, whatever they are, are unrecognisable and, 'ergo,' indecipherable.'

'Not necessarily,' she corrected, 'not if there's a pattern to them. The problem is the absence of a crib sheet.'

'How come you know so much about it?' I said, slightly startled.

'I saw that film about Alan Touring.'

'Pity he's not still around.'

'No worries,' said Verna, 'I bought that book of his afterwards so with luck we might be able to come up with something. Just give me until tomorrow to get over my singularity lag and we can give it ago. I'm going home for a bath and then I'm going to bed. You can always spend the evening making a start. Stamanana.'

***

I could have, but I didn't. Instead, I waited until the following morning before I picked up Verna's green drink tab again. She'd said that there might be a pattern to it; but how a pattern could come through so limited a text was beyond me? There was just as much of a pattern in, say, two cafe expressos and a wafer biscuit @ £14.80. So, I figured it might just as well be a bar tariff after all and decided to leave it until Verna arrived with her Alan Touring manual.

She wasn't long and had with her what looked like a stockist's portable bar-code reader, circa Pick'n'Pay 1999, and a manilla folder.

'Did you find anything to help?' I asked, frankly still sceptical how even a pointy head like Touring could help decode something flimsier than an old bus ticket from the other side of the Universe.

'Obviously you have to start from the Quantum field,' she began, confidently enough, 'which makes sense for us, seeing as that was how we built the black-hole in the first place. Touring worked out that if you don't have enough data then you have to devise an encryption with even less. But as he did a sort of proforma one himself we can use that. Look.' Verna opened the manilla file and removed the doc containing Touring's model encryption.

'Innocuous looking thing, isn't it?'

'It's certainly that,' I agreed. 'Did he really write that?'

'Well not exactly. Actually, Philomena came round last night, and we put this one together ourselves after a bit of a session, but we followed his version the best we could. Anyway, so then you have to feed it through this default anti-algorithm decoder,' and she picked up the price checker and gave it a wave, 'which basically means that all its decryption metrics are put through the ringer.'

'Mathematically speaking,' I offered, trying not to sound cynical.

She then took 'Touring's' pattern and fed it into the machine, which gobbled it up hungrily, like a domestic gas metre used to consume shillings.

'That's done,' continued Verna, 'it's obviously in a state of such high alert it could now decode a 'wait your turn ticket.' Only one problem, the program's life expectancy is incredibly short, about the equivalent of an anti-matter quark to be precise, so you have to be quick about it. Now where's that message gone?'

'You mean the green drink tab?'

'That's it. Now scan it here on the reader.'

I did as I was told, but to no avail, apparently.

'You have to be quicker than that,' said Verna, instructively; 'now I'll have to reset it. Give it another go, and don't schlep on it, like before.'

But it was still no good. Try as I might, the blip of the quark's short life got the better of me; and it was only after following her recommendation, of anticipating the scan ahead of the setting, that we finally got the read-out we hoped for. It went:

Hey Verna,

How are you? It's Max – hope you still remember me. We had some great times together, didn't we? Anyway, glad to see you got my message. Passing it over to you like that, so casual and perfunctory like, I guess it could have ended up in the trash! But I must have known you better than that Vee, as it has to be in front of you. Huh?

First off, you must know that I always took your virus hunt seriously. In spite of what I may have said at the time, not many people manage to build their own black hole and then pass through it without GPS; and very soon in I thought to myself, 'Hell! If you can show that kind of tenacity, then the least I can do is help bring it along.

Maybe you guessed by now that taking the virus back with you, undead, so to speak, was not the greatest idea; so, what you really need at this moment in time is a vaccine – am I right? Obviously, I could have produced one for you right then and there, but it would have been like leading you guys by the nose, and the last thing a Master of the Universe wants to do when dealing with the little people is come over all hubristic! Joking apart, what I decided was to pay a visit to those fellas who had already developed the perfect specimen to zap good and proper what you call Covid, and they call something else, I forget what.

Now that would be a feather in your cap, because as far as I can tell the way things are back at the ranch, (nb: he meant Earth, having lapsed for some reason, known only to himself, into Wyoming, circa Little House on the Prairie. V.Ed) – vaccine-wise, it's not looking too promising. No siree. It's the perennial dilemma I'm afraid, anchor punch the blister at 95%+efficacy, then give it three months and the little swell has only gone and multi-labyrinth itself into squadrons of new variants, more virulent than ever!

So, there we are Vee! And apart from all the diversions we enjoyed on the way (boy!) and our further penetration (gasp!) into their geography and society, in fact the main reason that we went to Icarus and the planet of the LGM was to get our hands on a vaccine that'll go the distance. That's what I was busy doing when I tooled off to buy the drinks. In fact, there was a bit of a schlep even then; most of the people in that quadrant are mercenary little snots at best of times and the LGM are the very worst, refusing to have anything to do with what they prosaically call a rank 'off-worlder,' unless he divvies up on the elixir which would deliver them into the psychedelic chromosphere of their rivals. I can't say I took to any these people over much and I really rather over-reacted I'm afraid. I just said: 'no deal frog-face, we'll finish our drinks, then we're out of here.' I was that put out Vee, I can tell you; and even though I could have knocked up the code for what he wanted then and there with brass braid on it, that wasn't the point – I just took umbrage – bunch of pills, the lot of them.

It was only when the red mist cleared that I realised how much I would be letting you down if we arrived home empty-handed, all because of a silly tantrum. Anyhow, before we left, I pulled off what I hope you'll agree is a bit of a sleight. I tip-toed over to a table full of their multi-coloured nemesis' and told them I had the specs for a digital app to download mega-volatile green melanoidal tincture which I intended to sell to the LGM for very many camels, unless they gave me the formula for their aka Covid vaccine – which is, if anything, superior to the one developed by the LGM. Of course, they fell for it even though I obviously had no such thing, such was their fear of conceding superiority over their rivals, upon which their supremacist national psyche depends.

So that's what you have here Vee, and if your clever people have decoded this far, then the rest of the formula will be a cinch. And if they don't make you 'World Queen,' for risks you've taken on behalf of humankinditity, then you sure are all facing darker days ahead.

Catch you later, Max.

REUNIONE

Those elements and gases prevalent in the universe which combined and compressed to form the stars also came to constitute the planets which make up the star's solar system. However, for those orbiting 'Helios', it very soon became apparent that only planet earth could be suitably accommodated with an atmosphere, as those too close to the sun were either starved of precipitation and moisture or corrupted by toxicity, (or both) while those furthest removed were too gravitationally remote from their star to benefit from it as a sufficient source of energy, and duly froze. The location of the earth, on the other hand, proved to be optimal and consequently it would enjoy an atmosphere which was sustainable.

Thus, the timeline with which we begin is just shy of 4.6 billion years; by which time nascent matter particles had bonded and gases condensed into this great emergent sphere. Generously, 'Mother Earth' assumed responsibility for sorting out her own geology and geography downstairs, while above it attended to an atmosphere of (mostly) benign, interactive gases, swirling and rushing as immodestly as the first oceanic currents. Still, the earth cooled dramatically under this gaseous shield, and it wasn't very long before the first life forms, albeit sub-bacterial ones, started to appear.

Beyond this, the combination of evolving atmospherics responsible for the world's climates and weather patterns and the undiminished energy emanating from the sun, has guided us through the evolutionary stages of life to the place we find ourselves at today: palaeolithic man coming to the end of his apprenticeship, already fired up and raring to go.

He came transported by gusts of solar winds, pockets of gas, held between spikes of ice and crystalline rock; oceans below, storms above, rivers cutting into mountains, younger mountains rising above those that came before. He landed on a patch of ground with a bump, losing touch on the instant with all these antecedents. Not stranded though.

There's blue sky and sun, clouds and rain; he's warm, wet, breathing the air, and there's clear, open space. Free, he extends his elbows in celebration but then finds himself hemmed in; there are limits after all. Dense forests tower above him; it's time for action. He rolls up his sleeves and sets to work, others join in. From the edges, inwards, clearing away at the margin, a piece at a time and a lesson learned. Later, there are fields, crops growing, a wide-open landscape that he's created, won in the war with the forest. In the distance a river, tiny tributaries criss-crossing the plain where he stands, like the capillaries in the hands of those who wielded the axe; and there's the village where he lives. It's perfect, idyllic, and wrong as if his carriage from the stars has been too swift and left him mis-assigned. Great forests at the perimeters still glower, beasts prowl and other men threaten, envy his freedom and look to check it. Nothing else for it then but confront it. He's faced adversity before and will do so again. Threats are there to be dared and overcome; as long as the enemy reveals itself, it can be opposed: but he's floundering.

What can it be? He puts it about in the normal way, but it comes back. He has a handle on most things, perennial, habitual things, kicking off from time to time, as they do. Is it really so hard? Hasn't he evolved master of his kind, with credits? He suspects a more unwonted, insidious enemy, one that mysteriously weaves in and out the strands of his consciousness rather than show its face. Except! - Just as suddenly he dismisses this line of thought and reproaches himself as if a mind probe is going to do anything to help him here. He rips out a clod of earth which he holds up to the heavens. It's plain as day; 'it's this damned weather,' and another crop failure in the offing. Before, his prayers were always answered, now the gods are not listening. The seasons have become untrustworthy, misbehaving. Floods follow storms, followed by droughts. Either this year or the next there won't be enough here to eat; all will fall to ruination, starvation, death. Any survivors will move on, nothing will remain. It's a depressing prospect, a life repeatedly threatened with no life at all. The end.

Time to emerge from the pit and muster in the communal dive, scooping out a stein of fermenting stuva; that's where his best thinking is done; their symposium. Hollow eyed, others will soon appear, fellows, wives too, children the only absentees, though it's their future to be decided. Later, there may be the chance to give that old lamp a rub, summon the genie within. He's a fickle, moody old so and so, but needs must....... Meanwhile, it's time to propitiate the gods!

***

The gods are upset and conspiring against us again, said Hep. We don't have corn enough for the winter and some of us will die; we should have heeded the warning two years ago when we survived only by hunting enough meat. This year is worse, and that option is closed as the deer have not returned. This is why we must mend our ways; we have become lax and sclerotic, perfunctory in our duties, to the dishonour of they who give us life. Now the sun ripens our corn then sears its goodness to husks before its time; the earth is starved of moisture then the rains return to torment us and flood our fields. There is no health in our land and there is no health in us or our propensities.

I see with my own eyes how the Great Temple to the Sun is neglected, said Eli. The way is clear for us to bring ourselves to bear and pay homage. Many will die this year but far better to die giving prayer to save those who will come after us. Going forward, we must make good the drays and the work animals and return to the quarries once more to hew out the great white stone; drag it ourselves if we have to, though you be on your knees for weakness and futility. Guard well our craftsmen and feed them up so they can rebuild our temples to the heights of their splendour. Most of all, keep our most coveted apart and prepare them for sacrifice.

I have just returned from where the great cloud looms above the high hill said Pez, where the earth is soddened by the cleaving falls cascading from the great rains. Herein the oracle dwells. It cannot speak for the Sun but does have words for the water, so sacred to its heart. It sends its message from the deepest hollows inside the earth's bowels. Its temper is short, and its mood scaly; it knows not the words for what pulls it one way, then the other. The rains hover, low and stormy; they fill the depths and hollows to the brim and beyond, and the earth above wallows, beyond lush. This is not true in other parts, far away; the labyrinth tells it so. It tells of very many hot lands, so much hot earth, baked, furrowed to a vitreous crust, crystalline hard. It tells too of great rivalries, monster water courses, hegemonies of them, crashing into one another, annexing each other's tributaries, drowning their streams. And at the edges, salt, salt and more salt. Everywhere salt. I asked the oracle where its pain was, so sad did I become. I asked again, to no avail, if it would help if we cleared away some of the salt. It just seemed the right thing to say.

I remember how our ovens roared and blew for all the goodness and abundance there was to cook; and all it lacked was salt, just a pinch of it, but none was to be had, said Jay, with sad irony. The children are older now, they have already lost interest in most everything else; their lives are tied down by the knots in their stomachs. They have stopped playing outside and curl up close to me, though now they are too old for me to feed; they will die first, after the old ones. Kay said: I don't allow mine outside anymore, the country is not to be trusted. All our herds cower, locked down in the stockade, filled so full that it would come away at the edges. My husband was attacked defending it from the wild animals of the forest, including those new monsters in all probability; it's easier fare for them than hunting deer, but they do that as well. I have no children, said May, with familiar dolour, even though I am older than both of you. I vote we sacrifice a single baby to ask the gods for extra fecundity; that way we will not only placate them but also have more hands to work the fields and more heads to fix all the other problems.

More mouths to feed too, chirped the chorus of all souls.

These are clearly unprecedented times indeed said Hep, (standing now below the great ivory bone held above his head by twine. It alone bestowed authority, but he kept a smaller version about his person, which he liked to wipe on his sleeve from time to time.) It is quite clear from what we've heard that our gods are out of sorts, and not only that, but they are also all equally displeased even though they have different sorrows to tell of. Now it's to all our gods equally that we should attend, I'm sure there will be no dissension there; but I also have something radical to add. I believe the cause of all these recent discrepancies and conflicts is down to the emergence of new gods; not to rival our existing ones, you understand, but to add to their story, to our story. Their distemper may be due to causes we are not yet able to understand, even they themselves may have their own doubts, teething troubles, I suppose you might say, if they are unused to their omnipotence, which is to be understood in the early years. The point is that it's up to us to learn their ways and respect their divinity, for it is to that sacred state to which they will ultimately be heading. It may sound extreme, revolutionary even, but facts must be faced, and I'm sure that we'll soon get the hang of it. The monsters the oracle told of gives us a clue. The scene is changing; we should never doubt our gods change too, always for our protection. We don't have to isolate any one for veneration above the other at this stage, however, to get the ball rolling I would like to nominate those giant fish birds that build their great nests so high in the trees. Each evening they return to the spruit, God warriors of land and sea alike, cackling raucously homeward, despite the serried rows of voracious pike, primed like sentinels, protruding out of their pendulous bills. There will be other gods, mark my words. Should we discover that libation and sacrifice are not to their taste, then we will lay those traditional rituals to one side; all the more pious devotions in the trough for the old masters, the first team fixtures in the Hall of Fame, you might say! All it takes is a co-ordinated approach. In fact, now I come to reflect, I cannot think why the answer never occurred to any of us before, though sadly too late for those of us who will never see our world pass beyond its next full cycle.

The view prevailing in the spiritual community, said Eli, is that we worship the Sun, above, but not to the exclusion of, all other stars. While this is well known we need to remember what happened in the past when arbitrariness reared its undesirable presence amongst us, with certain priests forming themselves into coteries, masquerading as saviours themselves, devising populist theologies and simplistic solutions to complex problems. So, our glorious star was expropriated by them, and they became a tyrant, demanding the punishment of those who loved the wondrous curtain of starlight displayed by the night heavens, or the marvel of reflected or refracted images mirrored in each and every single crystalline particle of our daily lives, castigating them as heretics or Helios deniers. What Hep imagines to be progressive, we discovered years ago? However, no need to go chasing hither and thither for fashionable new gods. The Sun nurtures and nourishes us; it warms us and brings us joy. It inhabits the very day in which we exist, where we live and work from the first to the last moment. Its tableau is the sky, which then starts to undrape itself as dusk descends and the heavens are revealed in their full glory. We are sometimes chided for failing to have the words to tell of these night wonders adequately and I would accept that as partly true, for even 'awesome' cannot do it justice. To my way of understanding, such demarcation is wholly irrelevant; suffice to say that our greatest forebears once described the dark hours as a time of grace and humility, but would forbear, if you will pardon the pun, to talk of the heavens at all.

Pez said: When I was younger, we fished in the fast mountain streams and played and swam all day. Even if there was a storm so the sky cracked and the rains burst, we laughed and cheered as, for a while, day became night. Sometimes the sun never came back, and we slept through the long night until the gushing water fell so silent you could just hear the plip, plip, plip of raindrops, as the day finally returned a little of its light. All then were desirous to see the sun again, but if there was more rain, spirits were downcast, wet as the earth, even inside our house where the roof leaked, as our very bed covers where we slept, as the grain store where our bread was kept, with the apples and greens gathered from the last season to see us through winter. Then we would stay out the way of the family who moped uneasily about, knowing that after they had done what they could indoors, that outside, in the fields, would be a long rescue mission just to save what they could. But we survived those dark days because we always trusted, we always knew the sun would return and teach us the water was still our friend, and had maybe misbehaved a bit, but had now learned its lesson and would be doubly anxious to please, at least until next time.

It just goes to show, said Kay, how the tables are turned. Our sun is always dependable, to breathe on us, friendly and warming, but now our rivers, and the rains that feed our land, are breaking away. I don't know if the gods are reconcilable, that's for our priests to tell us, but every sense tells me that they are more than flexing their muscles. How else can we take in what the oracle said, where the rivers that enrich our earth and rains cleansing our bodies now buck with monsters and giants. Some of them might be gods, but as for the rest? How are we supposed to tell one from the other? Those same fearsome creatures we tell our children about in fairy stories, and which I never believed in even then, are now here with us, so we're told. How can we hope to understand any god who seems bent on destruction, let alone assuage them? May said: giants slay little children by placing them in the palms of their hands then rubbing their hands together; ogres beguile them into dark forests and take them home for supper. You can bet that there will be raging falls and great floods as a result of these gods and their new dominion, but the solution is the same as always, only this time, more than any other, we have to rise to the occasion by matching their ambition and driving the sacrificial lamb sheer over the rapids, where we may assume the river gods reside.

No doubt in your devotion to the cause you would be the first to demand a place in the van of any such craft carrying the hapless victims you call the sacrificial lamb over the edge to paradise, thought Kay and Jay, and quite a few others.

Our plight may be serious, even deadly, but if our traditions tell us anything, then in the first place they warn us away from the temptation to resort to drastic solutions, and in the second, that in a crisis, our spirits always lift us. 'We have prevailed before,' might almost be our mantra, so frequently does it appear in our lore; and 'we shall do so again,' a time-honoured maxim, but none the less true for that. Let us all agree that our rivers are in bad humour, that's why they are in flux; and the rains that feed them must feel the same, as the seasons which used to mean everything for us, for them too, now appear to be going awry, so we cannot tell which is cause and which effect. This was Hep's provisional conclusion, with much still to discuss.

Our House counts all these changes, said Ford, that is myself, my assistants and all my fathers before me. Our seasons have been so defined mainly by reference to the length of our day and the warmth we enjoy, thanks to the generosity of our benevolent sun. Here we find that there is little seasonal variation in the hours of sunshine from year to year, while the pattern of rainfall is far less consistent as regards both its time of arrival and magnitude, as the seasons follow their annual cycle. Nevertheless, though totals can vary considerably from one year to the next, over the longer term, these tend to even out; except, it has to be said, our most recent experience has shown a small, though not insignificant increase in rainfall. As a caveat, can I add that even this is not unprecedented. Our annals confirm the existence of previous phases which have been similarly excited by aberrations in rainfall, some greater and others less than the annual average.

Arc & Pi said: As regards differentiating cause and effect in these and similar variables, we are broadly of the opinion that unless we are able to properly model that which we seek to explain with plausible assumptions about the real world derived from reliable data, we shall, sadly, fall short. Alas again, in no field of our endeavours is this the case more than our study of weather in all its aspects. Though it impacts us all the truth is that our understanding of even those of the world's elements which exist for us in a steady state are limited to informed speculation, so for any phenomena that lack stability, of which weather is probably the most universally pervading in our daily lives, even our assumptions are more than likely to prove questionable, let alone our conclusions! About all we can say with any certainty is that our weather is fickle.

The art of governance is guidance, said Hep; where we are unable to deduce, we can at least correlate, and regard non-irregular patterns as acceptable evidence, in some degree, albeit our best endeavours, for now, may only be second best. However, even the lowest rungs may attain their platform in time, and while our thinker's debate, our mathematicians calculate, and our adventurers make new discoveries, we shall not be found wanting in acuity as we summon our common will to grapple the next precarious step up the ladder.

Eli said: This is all irrelevant minutiae which invariably comes spinning out as soon as we lose sight of our true purpose, which is to serve and revere the bountiful gods who give us life; that same span of time which we now abuse by talking endlessly of whether this thing is or isn't caused by this or that other thing, or whether our rains arrive earlier or later than before or after. Truth is not to be found by positing this or that working hypothesis, or from tautological mathematical proofs; it is revealed to us by our faith, a word, by the way, which I have yet to hear in any of these purposeless reports. All else is deviancy, and if you are correct in a single one of your observations it is that they will be repeated again and again whenever we disconnect from God.

Woet said: Although I am joyful beyond measure to return to my home, my family, and friends, at the same time I am sad that we find ourselves in such troubled times. I trust that we do not despair, and God willing, we shall pull through relatively unscathed. My name is Woet, and I would like to tell you of my travels, my adventures, and the people I have met in lands far away, some of those same lands indeed from which our fathers came many years ago.

When we departed, we were advised to travel in the direction of the rising sun, so that we might discover the way round that Great still water that we would otherwise encounter if we marched straight ahead. I have to say that we were not successful; defeated not by lack of ambition, for many miles did we trek, but by the infernal marshes into which our natural pastures led us; without a sign of drier land beyond, and deterred as we were from seeking a passage round by the alternative way of the setting sun from other travellers' tales of hazardous swells of water which had long since drowned any passageway, or even neck of land. Thus, we were only able to continue on our way after we had constructed a sturdy craft to carry us safely over to the other side.

We have ever known of the existence of this Great water, but it was the first time I have ever had occasion to cross it. If I tell you that we had sailed a full day, and night to follow, before we sighted the far bank then you will have an idea of why we term it: 'Great.' Not unexpectedly, once we had disembarked, we found it was much the same on the other side, with this exception: the marshes were almost rank with foreign encrustations, of which sand was by far the most common, and thankfully, the least corrupt. And as we continued, and the marshes dried, and the land and air regained something of their freshness, the astonishing thing was there was still no sign of habitation. We only later heard the reason for this from the folk we were to meet afterwards who gave us a new word for our vocabulary. It is 'littoral,' and is where the shore of the still water has degenerated by an excess of barren additives, not just sand, but also brine and other alkalis.

The rivers and the waters are the chaos of today, said Pez; their order is all gone, and tempers are short, which is why they deposit our lands with corruption instead of goodness. This means it is here we must make our prayers and build our temples, otherwise their powers and monsters will destroy us. Who knows? The Great still water should become greater still if our monster river monsters land there!

After the littoral we bisected the day and carried on straight ahead, continued Woet, not to say we didn't confront more wetlands as we proceeded, and many more diversions due to other irregular still waters, until they were at last replaced by good green pasture and the sun began to properly warm us. We travellers draw on long experience from past journeys we ourselves have made, but far more than that we learn from the tales of those we encounter, who themselves repeat the recounts of others made before them; and so, we are able to discover our histories from first-hand experiences and collate them in annals of great moment. There can be no doubt of how many tales we heard of our waters making great unnatural presences in one way or another. Great currents, formerly twisting and turning with mathematical precision along their familiar courses, driving river and stream ever onwards in such beauteous patterns, delivering their goodness to this earth, now changed utterly, forming malevolent undercurrents, so that maelstrom and torrents kick back as powers intent on death and destruction. Reports of river monsters too are rife, and not just from our oracles, who never let us down when we are in trouble, or forfend, mislead us, but also from those who have ventured far further than any of us. Giants too, great monstrosities, half turtle, half fish, and eels, grown of arms and legs, ten foot high with tiny heads and minds to match, who run and splash about maniacally in the day, and wail at night in the bayous. The worst are the giant blubber fish, with the heads of men and the teeth of the Hydra that have formed themselves into armies, and whose arrival in our very domain can only be a matter of time; and for that matter, I'm not at all sure how many of these dire grotesques we could contemplate considering as gods. None at all would be my view, at least until they put in an appearance becoming of a deity. Obviously, as a seasoned traveller I know to take most of these more extreme tales with a pinch of salt and regard them as, at best, exaggerated, and at worst, sheer inventions. Yet so frequently were the identical tales told from so many divers, attributable sources, geographical as well as historical, that I am bound to regard them as primary research data, and hence corroborated and true.

Arc & Pi said: Until such time that evidence of a single such specimen is produced, any number of reports can only corroborate each other, not the reality of their alleged existence; neither do they add to any lore to which we might usefully refer in helping us understand our current predicament, let alone offer any explanation.

What we do have evidence of is of our rivers rampaging in torrents and the perimeters of our lands shrinking as a consequence, said Woet. If we had the time to spare, which at the moment looks unlikely, then we could put together a group of worthy and intrepid adventurers to follow the rim of the Great still water as far as they could travel. We know that they would have to endure cold and hostile conditions but the information they collected would be invaluable. Then there would be no issue of corroboration or discussion of cause and effect. We would know from reliable eyewitnesses, the facts of the matter, which would then help us identify the optimum course of action.

If the group divided into two instead, interjected Arc & Pi, then if the first one headed to where the sun rises, and 'backed' by an equal degree, while the second headed to where the sun sets and did likewise; should they meet, it would confirm what many of us can at this moment only speculate, that we are now surrounded by water. Then the exercise would only take half the time; if not, they would return by the way they'd journeyed, over an unpredictable timeline.

As we carried on, and became used to the greater warmth, went on Woet, we found the land settled and the pastures cultivated, as the rivers and streams ran their course and did once more service them. Then the empty spaces closed, and farms became hemmed in; families too lived closer together and the villages grew almost until they bumped into one another. Our scouts sent toward both horizons reported that the land's fertility gradually diminished until not a tree or wild plant out of place was to be found, whereafter all finally disappeared into hill country; but as long as we bisected our two horizons the land stayed fertile, and settlements thrived. We saw men and women working their fields, practising more intensive methods such as 'division of labour.' But we also learned that where those numbers exceeded the space to live and work, then they were obliged to travel the inhospitable horizons to find accommodation.

This marked the limits of our long journey. On our return, we noted many migratory souls in our wake, eschewing the barren lands spoken of, even to the shores of the Great still water, where many were making preparations to cross, and learned of many more, who had long since made the crossing and continued to make sojourn bisecting the sun's horizons so far that the cold would deter others from following. It seems that they are either hardier than any of our forebears or are resolved to endure the colder weather way past the lands where we stay. I would add finally that we should not bother ourselves about any likely competition from these people; they had consistently fought shy of contact with other settlers and to my mind appeared not to have the stomach for any sort of competitive hostility over the land where they would settle.

Migratory patterns are closely scrutinised where the evidence is available, said Ford; we believe they correlate at least partially with changes in temperature. I have stressed before how tentative any of the conclusions must be we draw, due to the insufficiency of our historical records, which means we tend to give undue weight to variations that are merely seasonal, or just random over so short a time span. However, with that proviso properly chastening us, it might be the case that migrants are not so much ready to face colder weather but that it is actually becoming warmer. Certainly, if there is any change in temperature over the medium term, our readings suggest that trend is upwards.

Hep said: Many of these reports and advice have contradictory strands running through them which make it doubly difficult to agree what action we need to take. Still, our reason can be relied on to guide us, even if the questions to which we require answers will possibly never avail themselves to any sort of rigorous proof. Though I may not be a magician with numbers, I recognise necessary correlation when I see it, and in my opinion the one that goes to the very heart of these matters is that between the life that is granted to us, and our humility before the benevolent gods who grant it. Amidst all this complexity it all comes down to something relatively simple and easy to understand.

The children have, however unwittingly, helped us in our quest to understand our predicament and the fragility of life, usually by digging strange bones out of the ground, or just by stumbling on them when playing games. More than once, they have disobeyed us and explored beyond the periphery, (as children will do) even reaching as far as wetlands and new still waters. They described the scene as like a giant green pond full of fish, but when we went to investigate the best, we could confirm were acres and acres of knee-high Marsh grass. Though, Jay continued, let not one of us doubt the authenticity of the 'skull in the water' they brought back with them, which still had blubber in its nose!

Eli said: the only contradictions are among us; we have displeased the gods, so they have all come out fighting, to put none too fine a point on it. The only so-called 'division of labour' which we need to practise is between those who work in the fields to feed us and those who dedicate themselves to the establishment and betterment of our temples and oratories. The sun, the rain and the rivers give us life, the magnificence of our temples must tell them that we are all truly humbled by their munificence.

Which only admits that if we wish to be distracted by unveiling the most extravagant way to waste scarce resources, as if its progenitor were entitled to a grand prize for his discovery, then here, we could at least claim success. Indeed, went on Arc & Pi, there is an almost an unlimited supply of choice corollaries whose questionable consequences may stretch for golden leagues before their causal fruitlessness is apparent.

To illustrate, let us consider the case of a criminal, caught, apparently, red-handed, in the very act of committing some foul murder; blood on his hands and seen by numerous eye witnesses at the scene of the crime, leaving footprints leading up to the victim's door, matching only his boots amongst those of all men in the entire neighbourhood; and moreover, that this same 'perpetrator' was also an alleged serial killer, who, in his carelessness, had left numerous traces of his presence at the scenes of his other atrocities; a strand of cotton from a torn shirt here, a broken fingernail there, in his hurry to entomb the corpse under the flat earth; so that investigating detectives could celebrate the apprehending of the culprit, and the community, scared out of their wits over the duration, could at last sleep easy in their beds.

At this point, the timeline of the parable divides into two, between a virtually instant date of execution, set for thirty-six hours after the guilty verdict, and a more considered alternative of twenty-eight days, primarily to allow petitions for clemency, etc. In both cases however, at a third date, set in between the other two, there is another murder, bearing the very same hallmarks as all the others.

Ford said: We know the heat from the sun varies through the course of the day and that the angle of sun to earth changes according to the season to make our summers warm and winters cold. We know that precipitation across all seasons feeds our rivers, which in turn feed the still waters, and I have alerted you to our observations and tentative conclusions based on the volume of evidence we have collected over many years. What we have less understanding of is the air we all breathe. Although most of the time it seems to be of a stable state as we go about our lives, that is an illusion: it is in a state of constant unrest, with warm and cold currents discernible, apparently at random, and rising and falling, again according to patterns we are at present unable to read. One interesting development we are busy testing, (I hesitate to say 'fact') is a link between the sun, the rain and the air itself. This, we believe, creates spectacular currents we can now recognise, and at least give a name to, as 'convectional.'

But again, we believe that this is just a very small part of a much greater story and that air currents form high into the heavens, feeding into, and in turn being fed by, great tidal streams in unimaginable flow, and contained only by the magnitude of the very heavens themselves. That which is contained within this great expanse of space is deemed 'atmosphere,' and the understanding of their dramatic jet-like course through the sky is the study of 'atmospherics.' That the air which we breathe ultimately derives from these great forces in the heavens means we can assume that the earth's atmosphere has existed at least as long as life itself, and quite probably ever since the beginning of the world. In this wise I think it is fair to say that as we return to the 'day job' of measuring temperatures, rainfall, seasonal variations and so forth, the discovery of any sort of static state will not be the norm.

Naturally, we are far more successful in sampling data from other geographically accessible communities that exist in our time frame, presently reaching even further than the Great still water, than we are in gathering it historically, and as vouchsafed by such traveller diaries as read to us earlier. However, with this proviso, it is still possible for us to go back to far earlier migratory periods, and even earlier eras still, albeit with far sketchier data. The tracing of weather patterns that far back allows us to evolve a separate, though obviously related science – that of climate. As a general rule it will come as no surprise to the more enlightened of us that whereas the former measures vary constantly, within fairly well elaborated patterns, the latter is far more stable, certainly when measured over time spans such as the average lifetime of any one of us. Thus, if one year proves to be wetter than another, or we get a sudden run of very warm summers or cold winters, then this is entirely consistent with the normal volatility of our weather. As I have stated more than once, there has been an up-tick in rainfall over recent years, which is showing no sign of tailing off; similarly, temperatures have also been on an upward trend, independent of the actual hours of sunshine, which change very little. However, to represent these same variations as necessarily evidence of climate change is erroneous, as these, and similar patterns have both occurred before within the same climatic time frame, as affirmed by our most historic data.

***

You will remember me, said Durk, as a member of the team which accompanied Woet on his mighty travels. I saw with my own eyes how men were struggling to rebuild their lives in the face of an extraordinary and rapid deterioration in fertility of their farmlands caused by the corrupt deposits of the new wetland marsh grass engulfing them. However, the far-end widening of the Great still water to extremes beyond measure, and torrential rise in power of the rivers which feed it, is just one part of this alarming story. Amongst the people to whom I spoke, I do not misrepresent them when I say that the view which prevailed, held by a clear majority, was that the sun was becoming hotter and the rains heavier.

But whereas I return home to find my people debating what mayhem emanates from great swirling winds high above the heavens which none of us can see, or how many men we can afford to quit their lands so they may build ever more ornate and flamboyant temples to dedicate and appease our cantankerous gods, the people I left had already worked out a plan of action; a plan that addresses our plight directly, and have begun to implement it this very day on which I speak to you. No more 'plucking of the turkey' now, or ambiguous proofs from idle causes or endless correlations. We know what the cause is; why the waters and heat rise to corrupt our lives; and more important, we can act to reverse it and return to prosperity, which will, incidentally, be nothing but a history story to our youth, unless we act.

Indeed, 'corruption,' in its widest sense, is the ideal place to begin our journey, as its prevalence in our lands is also enervating our spirits, indeed our very souls. Yes, were these ordinary times, I know I would be trespassing way beyond my brief here, but patience, the metaphor is worth continuing. For it is the corrupt behaviour in our daily lives has caused all this woe; our exploitative and indulgent ways have bred the very retribution which now stalks us. I'm not talking about 'sin' here, (that truly is beyond my brief!) rather it's the sheer waste effluence we create and the malodorous vapours which follow as by-products; and it is the fumes and smoke which we add by the wood and turf we burn. Ironically, you may suppose, but here we really do have something which makes sense of our so-called atmosphere; not mysterious, ethereal forces, high in the heavens, or in a world of ideas suited for they who should know better than to indulge in fruitless speculation, but actual, physical particulates, which are presently starting to choke up, not just the air in the high heavens, but also the air which we breathe here on earth. It has built up as a bubble of baleful morbidity, enclosing us like a blanket, so our temperatures carry on rising and venomous clouds of acidic rains pour down to pollute our rivers and destroy our lands, and ultimately, our lives.

Unsurprisingly, the answer is as obvious as the effect of the noisome waste and noxious gases all about us: we must cut back drastically, as a matter of urgency, all burnings of wood and turf in our hearts and ovens, and return as much pasture as we can allow, away from grazing to the farming of crops. Less meat will mean less cooking, so saving some need for fire, but let no one pretend that this is going to be easy; winters will still be cold in our lifetimes, and it is for our community leaders to agree a fair system of rationing. It's a crisis of our own making and we owe it, not just to ourselves, but to the generations still to come, to take these drastic actions: It bears repeating that if we don't, then there will be no home for them to inherit.

Jay said: We thought this Reunion was all about finding a solution, not adding to our problems. So, we now have to burst out of a bubble that no one even knew about until five minutes ago! Without meat or milk, the strong will become weak, and the weak will die. At least they who report rising temperatures to us have a school behind them, said Kay, which strives to find proper answers in good faith; to give us sufficient patience so that we know to have no expectations say, about the next few weeks, or even the winter ahead of us. But at least they leave us alone to keep warm the best we can. May said: I've always managed well enough on vegetables, and I don't see why everybody else can't do likewise.

There is no incompatibility here, said Eli, quite the reverse in fact. The displeasure of the gods with we who walk this earth only by leave of their good grace, I might add, has been evident from the beginning; in fact, it's why we formed this convocation in the first place. How proper therefore that we begin to show our contrition by setting to rights the defilement of his bounteous earth which is so scandalously the result of our abuse and neglect. Let us be plain however, that one hundred such remedial actions, although necessary in themselves, will never absolve us from our duty to bend the knee; in fact, it just means that the list of our indiscretions is extended, as is the need to pray for forgiveness. Never before has there been such a dearth in this community; our shabby shrines and minsters are an indictment on us all and a stain on our very souls. There is the priority.

Kayn said: The adversities we have encountered with such regularity these last years have, as a consequence, meant that we have had less of everything to share between us; principally food, of course, but also clothing, extras for the home and so on; and while we have been diverted by attempting to defend our current living standards, there has been a simultaneous deterioration in both private and social capital to add to our difficulties. Normally we can call upon stores and savings built up during more prosperous times to tide us over and at least maintain our necessary stock of physical capital, replenishing them when things improve. Today, these ameliorative options are no longer open to us. Instead, at a time when our productive resources are becoming ever scarcer and more costly to deploy, we find ourselves solicited to redirect them to alternative uses, the productiveness of which are either negligible or speculative. How we decide to answer is of course outside our remit; our function is simply to underscore the comparative costs of the alternatives, which in our estimate are prodigious.

We all know that uncommon problems require radical solutions, said Hep, and let no one doubt that the cost of them will be high and enduring. But before we start digging down into the relative merits and demerits of some of the fundamentals here, I would like to affirm our commitment to fair play, so that, going forward, the greater burden will fall on those best able to shoulder it, and vice-versa.

Now it seems to me that any suggestion attaching to one or other of the alternative proposals under review that it is 'speculative,' a word I've heard on more than one occasion regarding its efficacy, should be dealt with straight away. Unless I am mistaken, I'm not receiving any significant negative feedback concerning our duty to the gods, both in terms of our need for personal humility and our sacrificial commitment to their palaces, so that it may be accepted without question as part of 'The Lore,' and to doubt that means effectively doubting everything there is about what it means to be human, and indeed, the very purpose of existence. The only caveat I would add is that if for any reason opinions should change, then we should all of us be quite prepared to revisit the issue.

Which leads me on to our duties as custodians of the earth, granted to us by their grace, and the second of the two issues, just come to bear, namely, our wanton abuse of same. Here, the question, and indeed the solution, I believe, can be divided into three parts. Firstly, do we recognise widespread and deleterious defilement as a growing problem; second, do we acknowledge culpability, and third, are the countermeasures proposed efficacious?

Perhaps an analogy may clarify what we have here, said Durk. When our own houses gather dirt and we fail to give them a thorough clean, we don't need anybody to tell us that we are being neglectful and putting at risk the health of our families. Or if we carelessly mismanage our farms beyond their optimum capacities, say, by exploiting marginal land to our neighbours' disadvantage, or increasing the size of our herds at the risk of pestilence and destruction caused by over-crowding or inadequate boundaries, however naive or innocent our intentions, then we would not be surprised to be upbraided as irresponsible and anti-social. Briefly, that is where we are now, and it has to be said, avarice, not innocence, is the principal cause. It's not too late, but the big clean up must begin straight away, as men are released from these exploitative pursuits.

However, to reiterate, the worst culprit of all is the practice of deforestation and the wanton destruction by fire of precious woods, and anything else which we can think of adding to the pyre. To say that this is essential to keep us warm and cook our food, misses the point. A practice so self-evidently despoiling, and contaminating needed to be contained from the very beginning and managed communally according to agreed criteria; then practices could have been developed to identify cleaner, more efficient alternatives. That never happened, which is why we find ourselves in the position we are today.

If we were to adopt such draconian policies in their entirety, the impact on the public purse would be unsustainable, said Kayn. Very briefly, any switch of labour from the productive economy to all non-productive sectors, including cathedral work, would see a decline in volumes likely to cause drastic shortages of food and other essentials to below levels of bare subsistence; even if we intervened with the free movement of prices to ensure more equitable distribution, we anticipate that there would be insufficient to maintain existing population levels. Emergencies are not unknown in our society; my predecessors for instance were in the past occasionally charged with raising a war chest to pay for our defences as hostilities threatened us. Then, while we faced our enemy, desperate for funds to arm our troops, the majority of other peoples looked on censoriously, relieved they had not become involved in such a conflict. Nonetheless, such moral judgements held no sway for the capital markets, who, as ever, would lend, subject to risk, wherever a profit was to be gained. But then the sums added up: two warring communities needing to borrow, many others with surplus loanable funds available, prepared to lend. Not so today. It's the equivalent of a war over the whole earth; a multitude of would-be borrowers, but no lenders.

Strange days; quixotic, capricious days; desperate remedies. How many times have we heard these sentiments tonight, said Hayk, so I won't be out of place offering a few of my own? Dig a little deeper, we are told into some of the policies on offer, but before any of that, maybe we could drill down into that flaky old 'public purse' and see what we find. We all pay in, some more than others, and we all take something out; that's how it should be, we're agreed on that. But now, with such unprecedented new demands being made, it's in danger of coming to grief. Imagine a year when we can't afford to educate our young or look after our old folk because we're all so poor we can't pay our dues, or what little money there has been spent on other things. The lesson here is that we must revisit our priorities and look at things afresh.

In a nutshell, it is proposed the fuel we need to cook our food and keep us warm is to be rationed. As to 'why,' I'm sure you will all have your own opinions, but that's not relevant here. In a free market of course, its price would rise, and the poor would lose out; but with just a bit of tinkering here and there we might be able to change all that. So, if we say to the forester, whose production, we may assume, is to be somehow regulated, 'sell first what is deemed necessary to our community buyers at even, i.e., fair prices (we decide!) and recoup your return on the remainder by upping your price to those privileged others first in the queue who are busy clamouring in the private mart.' Then, we'll take a good look at what is best for the rest of us. The community's representatives may either decide to pool their acquired resources and run communal kitchens and even provide warm accommodation for the neediest or set up their own direct outlet and offer the surplus for sale to the majority at an equitable price, which is our preferred solution. And if anything, the public purse will be augmented as the community's supplies would be acquired at cost price. Obviously, the terms of reference in any debate concerning existing public goods such as welfare and education have to take into account our changed circumstances; however, we believe that this will provide the slack to enable men and women to live comfortably and, more importantly, make the informed choices to allow them to do so. Hopefully, things should improve as we return to prosperity in the medium term: Jam tomorrow, I'm afraid, but that is where we are at. Let me just conclude by saying, should we decide to review or reappraise the wisdom of any of these commitments, then all bets shorting the downside are off.

Let our narrative be clear, said Durk, which is a great deal more than can be said for the air that we breathe, let alone the previous argument. We do not just screw up our eyes to alleviate all the fumes or hold our noses and turn away from the foul stench of despoliation; we carefully examine all evidence to properly understand the monster that lies within. Briefly put, and now we have stepped beyond the fairy story that told us we were made of clay; of all the elements we are able to identify, it is carbon which is most essential to life; and of all the gases, it is oxygen. However, as soon as we put to fire that which comes from below, or grows out of the earth, then there is a remarkable, but deadly transformation: the two join together into one or other morbid combination, corrupting the delicate air to oxygen balance necessary for life on earth, and may even fuse further with some other foul toxicant, such as brimstone, before rising up into the atmosphere, until eventually the entire earth is surrounded by a foul, impenetrable, black blanket. I do not recognise any conscionable case for the 'reappraisal' of immediate and drastic countervailing measures.

I'm thinking here, said Jay, that families themselves might be able bring about a better method of care and education in our communities than us paying for leaders to organise it. I don't mean by the support we provide for our children and elderly relatives in our own homes, we've always done that. If I've got the jargon right, I'm proposing to provide them as private, rather than public goods; so that we will be the guiding lights, just as it is for our young and old folk who are affected. So, anybody who finds themselves without work can retrain for a position as carer, teacher, or whatever, and that can be the main subsidy which we take on, in parallel with a banded system of prices for the service we provide, so that those in the most parlous circumstances pay less. Everyone else will be charged the 'normal' price, which will be set at cost, plus a mark-up sufficient to cover the remainder of our outgoings; schools and care facilities, obviously, but also our need to pay for supplies and the out-sourcing of those menial services which the majority consider essential. Kay said: might our home workers even make so bold to rethink our cooking regime. I should say we have become too carefree in our attitude to heating the food we put on our tables; the grossest of cuts never bother us, be it meat or offal, when preparing the stew, nor the poverty of vegetable we're happy to accompany them, such is the intensity of heat we transfer to the cauldron to broil it into submission. So, I say that more attention might be given to pre-tenderising our meat and rolling root vegetables before their inclusion in tult; all practices our Grandmothers taught us of course, but that we've let lapse through profligacy.

And I would urge farmers to look to improve their husbandry, which might equally be said to have been neglected, said Hep. Our animal stock is too often left to wallow in wet lowland pasture adjacent to their kraals in the mistaken belief that the grossest of animals make the best carcasses. The reality is that they are best kept fit and, on the move, uphill and down dale, to eat and sleep and spend their lives as naturally as possible for herded animals. Optimal crop rotation too has fallen by the wayside; leaving land to lie fallow only after so long that there is no virtue left in it. Again, all practices which we have known and followed assiduously in the past and neglected for too long. Are not all our different tales and observations this evening just an expression of the same malaise?

Hayk said: Another way of looking at our condition is that these worthy practices, summarily identified, are all benefits which can offset costs. In fact, this is true of most of the exigencies on the public purse; they are far better considered, not as direct spending costs, necessitating extra contributions from all of us, but rather as opportunity costs, which are far easier to defray. It leaves us into less parlous a state and allows us more scope to run our own lives and spend our money, making informed choices in a free market.

What I would like to know, said May, is why there's suddenly so much more water everywhere when the sun is supposed to be making things hotter? Surely there can't be more sun and rain at the same time. And how come it's all our fault for trying to keep warm in the winter, which, by the way, to my mind, are getting colder not hotter, and especially the one last year, and that other one three years ago. And anyway, isn't it all just a pin prick, the fires lit by tiny communities like us, when you think how wide and extensive are our lands which no traveller has ever reached the end of? Even if there were hundreds of other settlements, including some that might have grown quite big, there's all that room in space for the smoke and the smells to disappear into. Unless of course it's all hemmed in by this great blanket thing we're told now covers the heavens; not that anyone can see it, nor did anybody ever think of mentioning it before, like if it was a long time incubating and grew bit by bit, still no one said anything. Or did it just suddenly appear overnight? One minute we are drinking our warm honey-drink, (no more of that anymore!) ready for a good night's sleep, the next we wake up to find ourselves locked inside a bubble. Luckily that's invisible too, otherwise half of us, including me, would have long since put it to the hat pin. Also, if there's not enough trees, then grow some more, like we do everything else, so that's that part of the problem sorted too. That's all I've got to say!

Durk said: You must know by the heat in your own kitchen what happens when the flue gets blocked, or ravens build their nest on the top of your chimneys what the affect is in any enclosed space; smoke fills the room, causing your eyes to sting and making you fight for breath. That's because the fumes are poisonous, so naturally you have to run out into the yard to escape. But even then, though your kitchen is uninhabitable, at least until the smoke clears, the quantity of toxic fumes in proportion to the unaffected area is frightfully small; yet the effect on you personally is a hundred times more dramatic.

It's the same with the atmosphere as a whole: hundreds of homes, and thousands of communities, fires and stoves constantly in use, on an upward trend, ticking up even further over these most recent cold winters, belching stronger, thicker, filthier smoke and fumes and poison waste products ever upwards and out of sight to us, creating growing numbers of toxicants wafting into the vast collection of atmospheric currents high in the heavens, whose powerful streams and variegated semi-tidal ebbs and flows have been so graphically described to you. It takes only a very little to do an awful lot of damage. Now I know 'bubble' and 'blankets' and so forth engender strong images for us to digest, and the more controversial and frankly dubious they must sound, particularly if they are described as certainly existing, except that we can't see them. However, think on this: the reason temperatures are on the rise isn't because the sun's rays are making our lives warmer, if anything they are dissipated due to their inability to penetrate all the filth we've let off into the atmosphere; rather it's because all the smoke and fumes that now constitute the upper air cannot escape, so neither can the heat. Instead, it just lingers, and the more we go on adding to it, the hotter our world becomes. That is why I describe it as 'living in a bubble.' But of course, nobody tells you any of that; climate, we're told doesn't change, in spite of what we see and hear all about us. Most farmers I've met confirm that the rains are turning acid as our precipitation gathers to form rain clouds in this increasingly toxic atmosphere. There's no hiding place here; our climate is changing in front of our eyes, and we are the cause of it. Hence, there's no other solution than the instant acceptance of the measures I have already outlined to you at some length. This brings me on to my final point which is this; that to delude ourselves we can do this cost free, or somehow move them off the balance sheet is as heinous a crime as the very irresponsibility's which landed us here in the first place. They are not merely 'transfer costs,' to be passed on to someone else, or there to be 'defrayed,' into endless strands, so each single sliver becomes almost invisible. No! They can only be faced head on and endured; and whilst I would be the first to admit that I'm nothing other than candid in my assessment, I also like to think that I am the voice of moderation; for unless we act now, I fear other voices more extreme than my own will clamour in pursuit of far more radical, revolutionary agendas.

No one in our school would ever try to dissemble any of the data we process, said Ford, nor shrink from expressing a view regarding its significance. Just to be quite clear: we have always acknowledged that past data on recorded temperatures and rainfall have trended both upwards and downwards, while irregularities in hours of sunshine from the seasonal average are far less common. Furthermore, we have never argued that climate does not change, or tried to maintain that despite the inherent changeability of everything to do with our weather, that these will even themselves out over the longer term into an unchanging climate. Obviously, by its very nature, a climate will be more stable than the aggregated weather patterns from which it is derived, but in the final analysis, nothing that owes its existence to the earth's atmospherics, unmediated and wild as they are, and ever have been over countless aeons, could ever be static. Quite the contrary, and we would be the first to admit it, as indeed we have done whenever our opinions are counselled.

One matter we might be able to shed some light on, said Vu, is the increase in surface area under water reported to us, and as evidenced by the Great still water itself, which has widened beyond discernible boundaries, and in all probability deepened too. Now we know it gets colder as we travel to 'back' from either our sun's morning or evening horizons, independent of the season or the height above ground level. After a certain point all precipitation begins to freeze and eventually turns to ice, so forming into one great cap to either side of the apex. Then as exogenous temperatures rise, as is the case at present, this ice starts to melt, thus adding to the area of surface water which we observe. Based on this, our projection corroborates the earlier hypothesis that the land which we currently inhabit will very soon become entirely surrounded by water. If we are not now an island, we very soon will be. And although we are only beginning to understand the rise in still water depths, we believe the melting icecap is only augmenting other great swathes of waters across unimaginably wide areas equal to, or perhaps even greater than, the entire surface area of land. That they are salt waters, is our present belief; 'still' waters, they most certainly will not be.

Regarding the broader debate, our investigations seek to probe below the earth's surface as deep as we can, where, very simply, each consecutive layer of rock encountered reaches down to an earlier period in our history; so, by examining samples at each level we can hope to find evidence of conditions prevailing in those times, especially those pertaining to life. Just to set the scene, and admittedly mostly of academic interest, I can tell you that the very deepest probes that we have so far managed have hit on a number of rocks which we are wholly unfamiliar with, and that are quite unique in their constituent parts, most of which we cannot identify either! Though we will of course investigate further, we do have a theory, even at this early stage, that these specimens were formed by unimaginable combinations of heat and pressure at these great depths, as if they represented a sort of primeval analogue of the more untrammelled and moderate conditions that are apparent nearer the surface, and that we are familiar with at the present day.

However, it is necessary to examine later eras if we wish to find out anything about what that world must have been like subsequently, starting with those eras just before the earliest forms of life start to appear, and years, beyond fathomable measure, before our first ancestors began to appear. It is here we believe that we can add something cogent to the climate debate: If we accept that that the rocks discovered at great depths were forged at temperatures higher than any we've ever known, then it is logical to believe that the earliest life forms only emerged after a considerable cooling down at the surface. Here we can only speculate, but as we move to more recent times, we find some evidence that the climate has passed through a significant number of evolutions, and that by and large life forms have adapted; – adapt or die, you might say. So, we know that before our times many types of animals walked this earth, some amongst the quadrupeds say, either with very thin or slick fur when the climate was warmer, and others hairier, like some of the great mammoths we still come across today, with masses of fat and blubber, so they be suited to colder climes. We have yet to develop as a school sufficiently to speak so tellingly on smaller fry such as insects, or aquatic types, such as fish; a fascinating life-form incidentally, which identify from as far back as we can reach, elementary types starting very small, yet growing to great sizes, and all well represented in the variety we are familiar with today. But that will be another story. For the time being, it is just meet that we use the relevant parts of our studies to contribute to the investigations of our colleagues in adjacent studies. To summarise, there is evidence that our climate has never been static and has constantly changed according to no discernible pattern or law. Make of that what you will.

I see evidence of God's hand more clearly than ever, said Eli; our inadequate sciences can never provide any proof of what causes such traumatic changes precisely because they are servants, like the rest of us, to our gods' masterful regime. Now more than ever must we offer prayers for salvation.

We see evidence of a more mischievous God stalking our earth, said Arc and Pi, who is arrogant enough not only to pronounce teleologically on the causes of our alleged predicament, but who also insists on wielding the hand which purports to deliver us all from an oblivion of effluence, based on a more than usually banal presentation of a correlation masquerading as proof. Logicians as a breed are a pretty rum lot, I have to say, but even we would hesitate to show our faces were such vanity to be writ so large on them.

Hep said: I don't believe the impasse I am detecting here can be resolved by way of further elucidation at this gathering, and so it will be incumbent upon me to seek a settlement, and one which will be binding on us all without recourse. We shall proceed therefore in the customary fashion to present the dilemma to the oracle and ask for a definitive ruling. Implicitly, at least, a number of speakers have given notice of the want of good faith in their opponents, hence it's high time that we put that behind us and consulted the fount of wisdom we are fortunate enough to have so generously provided for us by the gods, particularly, as I say, with so many of those here expressing an opinion emphasising how far we have strayed from the true path. Pez, our worthy messenger shall be despatched forthwith, and we shall all await his return with acuity and trepidation.

***

Pez: - I took the pilgrim's way out of our village, the same one travelled by myself on innumerable occasions, as well as by countless flagellating mendicants needful of solace for their troubled souls. I anticipated more than the usual number of hold-ups on this occasion due to the universality of our troubles as dozens of bare footed ones waited patiently for their genuflecting brethren to make their way. By nightfall I had arrived at the tiny settlement where all who aim to continue up into the highlands may pay for a night's accommodation and a morning's provisioning before they brave the gruelling final ascent which lies ahead. Like the monks, most travellers prefer to go alone, but in the case of those envoys accredited to present themselves to the oracle, such as myself, it is the mandatory stipulation, quite above all the others.

I left at dawn the next day to an almost spare trail with my mendicant companions already stretched well out of sight, and though there was a tendency for one of them to suddenly appear in front of you, due to the hair-pinning of the path, if they got in your way, a well-aimed kick up the backside soon cleared the obstacle over the side, with none any the wiser, so to speak.

All is panoramic and wonderment early on as the scenery is splendidly arrayed with multi-coloured layers of heath and heather fully indulged by the early morning sun and embellished by wild flowering plants of all description, particularly in the spring and summer, perennials too, past masters in eking out a glorious living in the tightest of clefts between rocks whose clutch became more and more vice-like as the track climbed and weaved its way inexorably towards the cave of the oracle. Arriving at higher ground, the flora undergoes a step change as the familiar lowland plants are replaced by mosses and lichen, spread out like a plaid, where space and exposure permit, but further on clinging like limpets to every nook and niche they can spy as the great vertical rock faces overhang what is now barely recognisable as a path anymore, and with even more precipitous cliffs overhanging them. Now I am forced to clamber the remaining distance, chasing footholds and trusting the most precarious looking handholds, committing myself more and more to chance, as the need to stretch further to reach anything attainable means being unable to test its constancy. Furthermore, despite making this same journey on so many occasions, I always find by the time I gain these refined heights, it's never quite the same as the last time, or the one before that, and it serves to remind me that the truly perplexing part of the journey still lies ahead. For when eventually that final ridge is scaled, the damp, featureless ground of the summit will take me along any number of false trails, some leading to an infinity of sterile, tiny caves, which make no claim to sagacity after all, and myriad others, dead ends in their own right.

The confined plateau of the summit was now swimming in water and the fountain gurgled menacingly. Perhaps practised more than I knew, I found the oracle's lair with a minimum of fuss; however, this time, I was not alone. How in heaven's name flailing genuflecting monks attained this place I wouldn't even be able to guess, for if they did it with the benefit of divine help, and I could not see any other way, then they would not need to be here in the first place. There were at least three in the queue for the oracle's grace ahead of me, and this close in, it wouldn't do to heave the odd importunate flagellant over the edge, given that the sort of ruling I had come to ask for required a hefty shot of contrition on behalf of its solicitor. Who knows, maybe they had come to ask the same thing as me, which for some reason I wasn't too happy about either, as if it would somehow devalue the answer I received, third or fourth along. After all, given the existing community of woes, the answer, whatever it might be, had to be much the same. Didn't it?

At 5pm my turn came; the oracle spoke!

***

'For a start you've come to the wrong place;' it boomed irascibly, 'we do water here, as you well know from a couple of weeks ago; 'the Fount of all wisdom' you want is next door. But before you wander off, I can tell you this for nothing: not even the entrails of the bubblyjock itself would be enough for the kind of resolution you're looking for. What can I tell you, that 'the Fount' wouldn't? Your people don't seem to be irremediably bad, if I'm honest; being generous, maybe half and half. So don't imagine, I don't know what you're all going through. Basically, nature's a balance thing, you know don't take out what you can't put back; don't pour waste on the land or effluence in the water; keep the air clean and don't pollute the atmosphere. If you're more careful and diligent in the future you'll find ways to do this properly as your methods improve; for now, don't let anybody tell you can't keep yourselves warm or cook your food. The 'Durks' of this world are incorrigible fanatics, and these days there's no primitive lobby anywhere I know of that's free of their presence. What's more, unless you start to buck your ideas up and improve yourselves, they'll still be here in 12,000 years' time! They're Zealots first and foremost of course, always hanging around whatever 'crisis of the day' is dragging along in the old caboose, if you catch my drift. It's not often I find myself agreeing with logicians, but if there's one show, we should definitely keep off the road, 'going forward,' it's arrant dogmatists like them. Final thought: if 'gods' are your thing, keep with the Sun; he's as reliable as they come, and he don't have the baggage of some of the others I could name.

'So, hoof off and give your people that message, from me. But of course, all this is only 'obiter dicta,' the real heavy stuff can only come from 'the Fount' itself. The good news is that the answer is all contained in 'the Word,' so none of that fathoming of profundities, or endless debating majority reports, with a couple of dubious minority ones to follow and confuse things further. The bad news is that it's a bit further off than next door, and they are rather choosy about who they let in. My advice is to get started once your 'not so wicked' messenger duties are done and you have handed in the provisional ruling to your community, courtesy of yours truly. Then head to the far horizon, (either one will do) and when you arrive at the kiosk there, ask for an audience with 'the Fount of all Wisdom'. They will tell you they're overbooked and to come back later, generally once you have walked as far as the other horizon, and back again. Worst case scenario: you will have to repeat that journey it until eternity before they'll take you seriously; best case? What can I say? Mention my name and you might get it down to a quadrillion. But that's not really the point. Instead, think of it as a worthy penance Pez, and just to show there's no hard feelings, when you do finally get to 'the Fount' and hear 'The Word,' bring it back here and we'll see how your people have got on over, however many years it turns out to be. 12,000 or so, didn't we say? Though obviously it will feel a lot longer to you.

'If 'the Word' still hasn't got through to them, then no price, I'm afraid, on the prevalence of irksome 'Durks' on just about every case you care to mention. Just marking your card Pez, don't say you were never told!'

'Fair call,' I replied, after taking all this in, 'and don't think I'm trying weasel out of it, but I'm thinking, isn't the task a bit severe just to hear a single word. I mean it's not so momentous that it will take me quadrillion trips to prepare for, is it?'

'Au contraire,' replied the oracle, 'in fact it's a word comprising a mere four letters; but I don't intend by the use of the term 'mere,' to in any way denigrate or belittle its profundity, or that which you must endure in order to understand its meaning!'

'Then,' I said, hoping to maybe negotiate a compromise, 'can you see any flexibility here; I mean I do something for you, and you tell me what the word is, save me all that 'infinite number of trips to the far horizon and back,' grief.'

'Now you mention it there is something,' said the oracle, 'these mendicants are getting vexatious beyond a saint's patience. Crock them and you got yourself a deal.'

'I agree,' I answered, with alacrity, 'now what's the word?'

'Uh-uh,' came back the oracle. 'You are first.'

So, I set out once more with a heart considerably less heavy than before and determined to live up to these new responsibilities. And the more I thought about it the brighter I became. After all, hadn't I already seen off a fair haul of mendicants already on the way up? Downhill it would be cakewalk.

Off they popped, one by one, over the side, into one or other bottomless void, depending on which side of the path they fell from, until in barely the passing of half a day, I reached my departure point, more exhausted than you might imagine only because the slope of the final kilometre and a half, passing through that verdant ornamental blanket of moss and lichen, heath and heather, enjoyed a far gentler incline, so consequently the former method of despatch, or 'drop,' had to be replaced by something more direct and unfortunately more conscionable for those disquieted by the sight of blood they perforce must shed wielding the assassin's dirk, however justified they held their cause to be.

Fortunately, I was not one so distracted and as soon as I had cleared these lowland bodies out the way I raced straight back to the oracle with a veritable spring in my step to claim my reward. Unfortunately, in my enthusiasm I had missed a frankly cheesy double-cross, admittedly one-shot point blank out of a bazooka, and in slow motion.

'All clear on the mendicant front,' I reported confidently. 'Now, the word?'

'I beg to differ,' said the oracle, 'I can see one pair of them at least have made it as far as the wild flora, with another couple already on the first tee.'

'Well, that's obviously happened since I set off up here, I mean, it was clear when I started out.'

'That's beside the point; here and now, you are not keeping to your side of the bargain. The word shall be revealed to you only when you do.'

By now, I could see where this was going and realised, I'd been tricked. Downcast, I considered my options, such as they were. It seemed hopeless, and I was just about to engineer a plea to renegotiate the terms down from infinity on the number of horizon-specific return trips to 'the Fount,' when I suddenly had an idea, albeit a desperate one.

'Dog's chance?' I asked.

Luckily, the big dog bit, the oracle liking nothing more than a bet, especially where the odds were stacked in his favour.

'Very well,' he said. 'Answer this simple question: What kind of creature is a 'Snagglepuss?' Dog's chances remember, one shot and you're out.'

I racked my befuddled brains; I was only a messenger after all, what did I know? How I wished Arc and Pi were on hand, or Vu, it was right up their street. I didn't have a clue, I'd never even heard of a Snagglepuss, let alone ever seen one. Is it a rabbit, I thought, or a mole; then again it could be a bird or something living in the earth like a worm. One chance, after that it would be back to the eternal lonesome highway. What to do?

Inspiration sometimes comes from wide open spaces, I considered, and remembered the wide wrap of colour that adorns the countryside at the path's lower reaches. Always better engaged with on the way down, I might as well go back anyway and gather up a few provisions I'll need for the marathon ahead, should I fail to work out an answer.

So low in spirits down the now well-trodden track I made my familiar way back to base, and despite seeing off a couple of mendicants en route, it did nothing to cheer me up, and I arrived back where I had started, thoroughly cheesed off.

Covid Express

***

Inside the little shop their things at last started looking up, for in front of the fire, sipping a mug of tea, sat quite the prettiest girl I ever laid eyes on.

'I'll be with you presently,' she said, 'just let me finish my drink;' on her knee, purring happily was a tiny kitten.

'What do you call him/her/it?' I asked, somewhat maladroitly.

'Kitty,' she replied.

'What's the matter with her fur?'

'Oh, you mean where it's all snaggled up? It's nothing, it will come out with a good brush.'

'I don't think I know that word,' I admitted.

'No, it is rather peculiar isn't it,' she agreed, 'like a snag followed by a tangle; it's quite common though.'

'Remarkable,' I thought, out loud.

'Now, what can I get you?' she said, getting up, putting Kitty to one side, and going back to the counter.

So glumly, I gave my order, as my mind raced ahead to the rather horrible task ahead after such a pleasant diversion. Reluctantly I said goodbye to my new friend, and boldly gave her a quick peck on the cheek in spite of such a short acquaintance. Perhaps we can pick up again when I return, I thought optimistically.

So once again I made my way back up the path; I would just have to admit defeat; there was no inspiration from the magnificent views on the way down, so the chance of a last-minute revelation on the way back up were as near to zero as made no difference. I certainly knew all about zero sum games by now! Then just as I was bowling another mendicant over the edge, to keep my hand in as much as anything, an idea did actually stir somewhere in the cerebral back office. Already I was closing in on oracle territory, so anything was worth a try.

As I came up behind what would probably be the final mendicant, so close were we to the top, the hapless fellow turned to face me, as if predisposed to his fate.

'I'm ready to meet my God,' the mendicant said, getting in first, given they might be the final words he would ever utter.

'We don't have to do this,' I said. 'Instead, I can offer you a 'dog's chance. Answer me one question correctly, and I promise to leave you in peace.'

'Very well,' said the mendicant, suspicious, in spite of the serendipitous get out of jail card.

'What is a Snagglepuss?'

'It's a cat.'

'You're sure?'

'Without the shadow of a doubt.'

'Very well, 'you may be on your way. Butter up the oracle while you're at it, I will be right behind you.'

Mendicants generally regard their life on earth as spiritual preparation for the heaven that awaits them; still, you could tell by the sprightliness with which this one bounded off that he was more than a little determined to shake some more action out of this one first.

'A cat, eh?' I reflected in wonderment, 'who'd have thought it.'

Twenty minutes later, I was back outside the oracle's cave, head of the queue. Soon it was my turn, that very same mendicant just emerging, a bit queasy looking, it had to be said. So soon after his reprieve, I mused, the oracle must have given him a real stinker.

I made my presence known with a delicate 'ahem,' and the oracle groaned from somewhere sepulchral, sounding like he'd been on a five-day bender.

'Well?' was all he said, by way of acknowledgement.

'A Snagglepus, Remember? A dog's chance?'

'I remember,' conceded the oracle.

'If you had a drop of sporting blood, you'd give me a three-shot.'

Oracles shouldn't be that easy to rile, after all, they had risen to the top of their profession. But obviously the cure hadn't taken, and he rose to the bait.

'Go on then,' he leered at last, 'not that it'll make any difference.'

'Is it a bird?'

'It is not.'

'A fish?'

'Nor a fish,' sneered the oracle, evidently feeling a bit better as my chances dwindled. 'Now you're back where you started, ars-wipe.'

'Then it's a cat!' I went triumphantly.

Cue industrial scale oracular tantrum. Nobody had even known that an oracle had feet until that very moment when he stamped them so hard that the floor of his cave gave way and he tumbled far down into the depths of the labyrinth, heading for the earth's core, but still managing to call out not to forget our appointment in 12,000 years' time.

However, by then 'the Durks' had taken over as the oracle had predicted, and planet earth, whose progress up to this point had been nothing to write home about, was now headed for a very bad place. Consequently, Pez never did manage to find out the 'word,' which was a pity, because we know it was only four letters long and conveyed a meaning as portentous as it was uncomplicated; it had even done the rounds earlier at the Reunion without anybody realising its significance. But once the tyrannical Durks' are let loose, spoofing crisis after crisis, and demanding everybody worship only their meddling gods, then I'm afraid its meaning just gets lost in the simplicity of translation.

The word is of course............

**

Men, are you skinny; do women laugh at you when..............?

Walls of Goldsithney

'Do you want to hear something extraordinary?' said Maria.

'Is it our holiday?' replied Ethyl, obliquely.

'Well obviously it's something to do with it, as we're down here now and I, at least, have been exploring.'

'Only because you left me with that woman who runs the place.'

Maria Despenser and Ethyl Smiles were on half term holiday in Cornwall and had just arrived at their cottage; it was 7pm on a late spring evening and Maria had straight away gone outside and walked the remaining few hundred yards between the front gate and the end of town.

You could see the line of demarcation ahead of you, as the school with its playground, the terraced artisan cottages, even the aged slabs of pavement, redolent of old industrial Cornwall, impregnated with kaolin, gave way to open fields.

Neither was this the only relic of the past as barely fifty yards out of town a sign pointed to a cluster of old mines with a warning for sightseers to be careful. Most of these were inaccessible anyway without excavation equipment, except for the one Maria went in where an old rail track still penetrated inside, with at least enough light to give a furtive investigation a sporting chance. It was the outcome of this visit which had made Maria particularly anxious to share the experience with her friend once she'd returned.

'It's in one of those old pits.'

'You've been down there already?'

'But guess what?'

'I don't know; we can see tomorrow.'

Maria sat on the bed. No one would call her excitable, but something had definitely touched her, only she was desperate to take Ethyl and show her rather than tell her the secret. There was clearly a disjunct here between her emotional intensity and Ethyl's total apathy and only direct action would work.

'You must come now,' she pleaded, 'it's only a minute, please come.'

'Well give me a moment to get organised then,' said Ethyl and having exacted this concession, Maria celebrated her victory by standing at Ethyl's bedroom door, right up to the point of delivery.

It was now just before 8pm and Maria's patience was wearing thin, such that when Ethyl did finally pronounce herself ready, Maria darted on ahead, reproaching her friend for her indolence each step of the way.

But finally, they reached the entrance to the pit and Maria pointed:

'It's in there,' she said, no less cryptically.

Ethyl bridled. 'I don't fancy that,' she said, 'not down a mine, we can do it tomorrow.'

'No, we must. It might be lost tomorrow,' said Maria. 'Come on, it's not far in.'

Ethyl had started to say, 'what might be lost?' when Maria entered, then turned to Ethyl behind her.

'Come on,' she beckoned, and Ethyl stepped tentatively in behind. Maria did not need to repeat the manoeuvre and only stopped again when she reached the end of the track where the little gallery was cut into the rock.

'This is the place; it's here,' she said.

'What?'

'Voices.'

'There's no voices, there's no one here but us.'

'Listen.'

'You mean that sort of hissing?'

'Inside the hissing.'

'You can't go inside hissing, like it was some sort of separate space with a door.'

'Just listen.'

Then she heard something, distinct enough to make her start, not a voice, an irregular wave of sound, but with the intonation of a voice; the second that became clear, a voice draped itself about it and she heard what Maria heard.

'No one was here before either,' said Maria, 'just me.'

'What's it saying?' hushed Ethyl.

'It's repeating itself, that same modulation, see?'

Ethyl concentrated the harder and finally discerned it, assisted by Maria's fantasy conductor's baton.

'Is it definitely words?' asked Ethyl, starting to give ground to her friend's better progress. Then almost immediately Maria said: 'Je vous something – it's French, and bateau. Hear that?'

'And 'Est ce que,' added Ethyl, 'and Spartacus, that was clearest of all.'

'Spartacus? That's mad.'

'It's certainly not French.'

'Where can these people be? They can't stay here all night.'

'There's still no one, and neither can we stay here all night.'

'But they'll be gone by tomorrow.'

'Well, we can't take echoes of voices away with us. Come on, the light here's nearly gone. Maybe something will come to us down the pub. We could ask the locals, see if they've got any bright ideas.'

'Like disembodied Bronze Age Bretons?' suggested Maria.

Being fully constituted members of the English school of everyday life sceptics, they set about discarding all the evidence of their own ears almost immediately, before returning to the crazy consequences of what they'd heard.

'You know it will all have disappeared by morning don't you,' said Ethyl as they were both scrambling back up the slope of the old mine, and both girls spent the rest of their way home amusing themselves making adenoidal whooshing sounds which they thought best translated the sound of a hiss into French.

The first pub they went in was so ghastly, void of all character except traces of local Kaolin in the carpet and yobs leering at them from bar billiards in the public bar, that they walked straight through to the saloon and out the other door. The one opposite looked no more inviting, like a Methodist Hall which had acquired a pub sign, but they entered regardless and found nothing more threatening than a pensioner with a pint and a retriever, and an innkeeper in shirt sleeves and corduroy waistcoat, busy shifting something in his ear with the end of a tea towel.

'Yes m'dear,' he said to Ethyl up at the bar, every inch the Cornish caricature of rural hospitality, tufts of curly grey hair above his ears, separated by a broad furrow of shiny sun-bronzed scalp, with anarchic, querulous eyebrows.

'Two small scrumpies,' said Ethyl, smiling back, grateful for the friendly reception: that was their local sorted for the duration.

'Down for the holiday?' enquired the merry spirit, as he pulled a pair of cloudy glasses.

'Half-term,' she replied. 'Thanks.'

Before she re-joined Maria, she said:

'We had a quick look down one of those old mine shafts earlier, has anyone ever opened them up?'

'Just exploring like,' he said, 'nothing much more. Don't go too far in mind, don't want to lose you this early,' and the gleam in his eye was accompanied by a rustic smile of russet-coloured teeth. Ethyl pressed on though: 'No ghosts and spooks we should know about then, from any old prospectors' tales?' she said, half-confidentially.

'None who've come back anyway,' he said, beaming wide enough to embrace all comers and especially those patron members of the 'locals would have more sense' club.

'Cheers,' said Ethyl, as she took the drinks back to the table.

'Hear that?' she said when she got back, 'nothing round here like that has been reported; if it's an old, haunted mine, he's never heard of it.'

'Cheers,' said Maria, and took a decent slew of cider; even that she could feel with just breakfast inside her from before the drive down.

'Do you want to hear my theory?' said Maria. 'That whole space is like a whispering gallery which somehow transmits voices from people further in who we couldn't see.'

'I thought that, but no one ever appeared all the time we were there; it couldn't just hang there for like an hour.'

'Well maybe it got stuck somehow and it was just those few French words always repeating.'

'There's got to be some law it contradicts,' said Ethyl, looking about her for inspiration, 'dissipation of sound waves in space maybe, some void in nature that abhors another one? Didn't know any sound engineers at Exeter, did you?'

Her friend shook her head with a knowing grin; somehow, they'd grown beyond ribald cracks at the undergrad engineering community.

'Let's look what we've got so far,' Maria went on: 'a few bits of grammar and two actual words, bateau for boat and Spartacus, which is just a silly name.'

'Apart from him, it's all in French, and there was no sign of any French people. Who is Spartacus anyway? I know he was in a film.'

'He was a Roman slave, BC sometime. Long before they invented French.'

'Wasn't he from the Holy land?'

'Thrace, I think.'

'I know he met Jesus in the film.'

'You're thinking of Ben-Hur.'

'Perhaps,' she conceded.

'But there's one thing I do remember. Our teacher had a map of the Roman Empire, and Thrace was always allied with Gaul.'

'So that would explain how he gets included with the French, you mean?' said Ethyl, sardonically.

'It's all we've got so far,' answered Maria, pithily.

The pub had in the meantime started to liven up as the evening unwound. A little party had gathered round the darts board, two fellows and their girlfriends, regulars, making straight for the chalk board at the end of the bar, lining up their dimpled pint glasses and absorbed instantly with the game; sundry others were greeted with a chorus of recognition from the landlord's corner of mustering yokels which had grown as the evening wore on. Later in the evening the landlord's wife put in an appearance for a stint behind the bar, spent texting on her mobile, while the landlord himself remained amongst his little coterie of regulars, distracting himself with the odd flick of his old tea-towel at some escapee from the blue cybernetic death-rays of the fly trap above the sandwich board.

Out of the window opposite Maria the dark had crept up the side of hill where the old mines were to merge into the moonless night. Still, try as you might, in a county replete with 'Old Jamaicee Inn' smuggling coves and baleful Lorna Doone moors, it wasn't easy to build a convincing back story to their 'whispering galleries' narrative which would fit in with the bland, ordinariness of this place, a kaolin blanched dead end of a town which gave up its unremarkable slate-coloured municipal buildings and schools to featureless new build estates down uniformly uninspiring cul-de-sacs.

Next day at breakfast they recalled their experience straight away, only to give the whole thing the full-on Hadron collider treatment of cynical disbelief, admixed with the counter-intuitive view which held that though it might have been bottled up for centuries, it would surely have evaporated by today. Along with a determination to return before anyone else got there they left home that morning with the gusto of children on a summer holiday, about to re-discover some secret garden visited on them the night before.

Relief all round: The hissing noise was still there, exactly the same, and they were still alone.

'The daylight goes as far as the other side of the gallery,' said Maria, 'let's see if we can make out an any more words: just go carefully.'

They watched and listened as they followed the disused rail track which opened further into the rock, with no precarious pit-props of splintered timber or creaking ledges to hamper progress. It was difficult to work out if the hissing had intensified while their bodies were in motion and when they reached the other side, they stood still to let their ears to retune. Very soon the familiar patterns began to return, and those same words could still be descried, continually repeating, though there were no new words to buck up the vocabulary. At this farther side the railway gave out and the track continued down a narrower tunnel dug into the rock; both girls walked as far as the entrance and stopped: it was dark, and to go any further they would have to stoop.

'Give it a go?' went Ethyl, fondling her cell phone intrepidly to access torchlight.

'Just an inch at a time then, until we see where it goes.'

But even an inch at a time soon brought them into a second recess, much higher and wider than the first one, and at whose threshold they received a jolt to the sensory antennae which would have knocked the average 'Ironman' clean off his stanchion.

The entire space seemed to have morphed into a multi-dimensional kaleidoscope of crystal, where diagonal shafts of light forked down from the roof, split through a spectral prism, like a full-scale replica of the 'Screen Gems' motif used in old movies. Then a wild rush of colours swirled and twisted in great colliding eddies of air, as though transmitted through drafts of formless smoke, and sounds rang out of every pitch imaginable; high as a celestial choir cast in the glazed ceiling, trebles duelling with crescendos of sibilance, low basso-profundos, simulating the murmurs of some gothic graveyard, gusting vortices of grey mist and ash, entirely without substance.

'Far f----ing out,' went Ethyl.

'Have you noticed her?' said Maria, indicating a not un-puckish figure sitting cross-legged on a large slab of what looked like feldspar in the centre of the space.

'Do you think she's meditating?'

'Ask her,' replied Ethyl.

'Excuse me,' said Maria, walking over.

'Oh hallo,' said Puck.

'We thought we might have startled you. What is this place?'

'I know, it's amazing isn't it. I still can't get my head round it, and I've been coming all season.'

'Have you seen anyone else?' asked Ethyl.

'Only you two,' she replied, 'since I found it this year. I study musical composition and I always came to Cornwall for peace and quiet. But all the sounds and colours in here, there's harmonies and echoes and all those waves and pulses, it's like some sort of multi-sensual auto-mixing desk.'

'How come the miners never found it?' asked Maria, 'the mines in Cornwall go back to the dark ages.'

'Or even other people on holiday,' added Ethyl, giving the question extra impetus.

'Sometimes old seams just collapse?' don't they, offered Puck, 'from loose sediment, only what's replaced this one is a space full of amazing lights reflecting off pure crystalline.'

'All those colours are found in minerals like onyx and quartz,' said Ethyl, recalling at least something from nature study.

'We came further in to try and hear some more of the voices,' said Maria.

'I know,' said Puck, 'they're really freaky, aren't they? And all those waves of hissing are even more intense in here; it's like that great crescendo that builds up as you get near Niagara.'

'Reminds me more of Eraserhead,' said Ethyl.

'What's Eraserhead?' asked Puck, unsure if she had any more unexplored wavelengths to probe.

'Some cult seventies movies set in a wind tunnel,' answered Maria.

'That would do it,' observed Puck.

'The voices are all in French, aren't they?' said Ethel, to Puck, 'and just keep repeating in that same vibe; is that what you've heard too?'

'I'm not sure what they are,' said Puck, 'I get as far away from them as possible, so I can concentrate on the harmonic sonorities in the centre. I've composed so much, it's like having your own lab out there.'

'So, what is it you're hearing?' asked Ethyl. 'To me it sounds a bit like plainsong, or those Gregorian chants.'

'I've composed plenty of them,' agreed Puck keen to share her passion, 'but after a while you can develop much more, almost like pan-dimensional chamber music.' Puck however was a wise enough old bird to know that an exegesis of the classical muse harmonising with vibes in a polyphonic grotto was not a journey everyone would enjoy sharing, so she left it there. Similarly, Maria held back from enquiring if oratorios or opera ever got a look in.

As the moment extended, the hissing magnified, and thoughts returned to the text and its substance.

'It's certainly a repeating lilt,' said Puck, now concentrating on what she had once neglected; 'I can't make out the language though.'

'Any more words?' said Ethyl to Maria, as philologist in chief.

'Je and de maybe,' she said, concentrating on the rising wisps of inarticulate air, 'I'm still certain it's French.'

'Then, compense, I'm sure,' she said. 'Is that a word?' Ethyl shrugged the 'search-me' look.

'Recompense,' said Puck helpfully, 'it means reward.'

After most of the morning spent in this fashion with the girls animated in conducting modulations, trying to coax additional narrative from the regular, pulsating atmospheric whistle, they claimed half a dozen extra words, only 'pricked off,' in the censual sense, provided they were authenticated by at least one other. These included, bon, prometre, blanc and garde.

'So, where's it coming from?' said Puck, 'there's no one here. It can't be boxed up in the walls, can it?'

'On that, we've not the foggiest,' admitted Ethyl; 'all we know is that we can hear it.'

'I suppose we could ask someone outside,' said Maria dubiously, 'not that they'd believe us.'

'And if we showed them, you can be sure that's when it would disappear,' replied Ethyl, philosophically.

'Then I tell you what,' said Puck, glad to recruit a pair of fantasy explorers into her domain. 'Let's just stay with it until the words make some sense; after all, we can all hear something, and it may have been here for ages.'

'Agreed,' they replied, persuaded by the upbeat sentiment of Puck's suggestion.

They spent the rest of that day and all the next in the psychedelic cavern. Puck came down from her lofty perch and joined Maria and Ethyl on whispering wall duty. They decided to split up and each examine a different section of wall, and in so doing were instantly met by the wall raising its game, as if in recognition of the extra attention it was receiving. What's more, the surface of the rock felt softer to the touch, almost malleable, as they each pressed against it in an attempt to penetrate its innermost secrets. So absorbed were they with this overt willingness by the wall to co-operate that they quite failed to notice that they had moved out of sight of one another.

It was then that things really began happening. A shaft of light from the twisting nucleus above drove down as a spear, enough to make Maria flinch, and opened the smooth granite rock face into an array of grey-green crystal, which widened and de-compressed, as if in relief at a tight rein loosened, and the whistling that had surrounded her and pervaded the rock fell back as the strength of colour gave greater clarity to the sounds it contained. Only passively was the beam extinguished, when, with a sensual wince, the granite wall reformed and the whistling resumed, as if conceding the return of its regular pitch.

As Ethyl probed the wall, the air itself began to weave and variegate its way about her body, as if anxious to mark her as one of its own, each strand differentiated, sensuous. The roof above and ground below now lost their solidity as mist rose and fell, playing with the atmospherics about the wall, which opened and gushed crystal azure in welcome. Its joy at the new purity of its acoustic was palpable, but short lived. Suddenly, a threatening waft of black cloud blew a shudder of gas molecules out into the recovering gallery and the air guttered with a temporary loss of oxygen; a hissing whistle screamed once, before falling back to its earlier pitch.

Puck's arc of wall simply collapsed amid a great army of peals, chords and chimes, which competed with exquisite dissonances to fill the space left vacant by the rushing, barbaric affront to pure harmony, assembling into a beautifully meshed cadential fretwork. Again, the giant space into which they all settled exhaled with wonder and pleasure at the replacement of brutality by art, while the great musical polyphony to which it was about to give birth, shimmered in anticipation. The sinfonia it chose to deliver, as a geo-spatial counterpoint, was so refined, that the terpsichore lamented its transience, as the hissing resumed.

Once the horizons returned, each girl picked up from where they had been at the beginning. If not sentient, then the wall had at least only released those secrets which it chose; and if somewhat unforthcoming on its methodology, quite understandably so, given the track-record of most of those with whom it had been historically forced to deal, it had at least issued a colourful working transcript of what it held within. The wall had intimated with each girl's mind separately in the only way it understood, by a sort of psychic osmosis, yet the message it delivered had, bar a few stray words here and there, been the same.

Translated from the French, it read as follows: 'Make sure you follow the plan; I will be at the port; meet me, meet them; the ship will sail; part of the promise; follow Spartacus; stop Spartacus; take care reward, success; return to England; remain in France.'

'You know what strikes me?' said Puck. 'Apart from a wall that bends dimensions and talks, I still don't get how no one else has ever come here? It's not as if it's hard to find.'

'If you wanted a mystical perspective,' ventured Maria insightfully, 'you could say that it operated some sort of psychic barrier to prevent people discovering its secrets.'

'Like a polyscopic sound repository with attitude,' suggested Ethyl.

'Didn't stop us though,' said Puck prosaically, returning to the dilemma. 'Perhaps if we worked out the meaning of the message, then the rest of the place might start to make more sense, distorted dimensions included.'

'And we might see if it had just been by chance that no one else has found it,' said Maria. 'I still really hope they don't.'

'Almost like we'd been violated,' empathised Ethyl.

With no other options gaining currency Maria and Ethyl left to study the text they had translated, to find some interpretation which made sense. So far all they had was the maritime context and an absence of names other than Spartacus, which made no sense geographically or historically.

Puck, real name Virginia Pinches, remained as Puck, and she also remained at her location at the inner cavern where harmonic wonders continued to come her way. Despite being in an old mine, the ocean was somehow making its presence felt now, rinsing all scales and tones with saline blue driving rhythms, pounding tidal dynamics and rising glissandos of salt sea breezes.

Later, she caught the pair of them on the beach; Maria was towelling off from a swim and Ethyl sunbathed, laying her lap-top to one side, having burned out diver's search engines on what little data they had collected.

'Anything?' said Ethyl, as Puck sat next to them.

'I thought this,' she began, 'ships cross oceans and pass-through channels, whereas boats cross channels.'

'Troop ships crossed the Channel on D-Day,' said Maria, helpfully.

'Exactly,' replied Puck, 'and have done ever since this country had a fleet of ships.'

'King Alfred founded the English Navy,' read Ethyl from her screen, having just coaxed out another unsuspecting search engine.

'So that gives us a historical context; before Alfred, people only had boats to cross with; after the end of World War Two, well, I'm not quite sure, but they don't seem to talk about ships crossing.'

Mary and Ethel swapped looks, but the temptation to dis Puck's findings was easily resisted, given the dearth of their own.

The sun was still baking down from its high solstice arc in spite of the lateness of the hour and the incoming tide gave one more petulant spurt to move them back up the beach. By now nothing remained of their little sheltered cove carved out of the picturesque rocky coastline, yet come the ebb tide, when the intermittent spread of elemental rock pools returned, it was difficult to imagine any craft trying to land safely, let alone one the size of a ship. As they made tracks and reached the top of the tortuous, narrow path which took them back to the top of the cliff, gazing out to sea, it became obvious how the smugglers, who reputedly thrived along this coastline, must have proceeded.

'Their ships would have anchored out to sea and never come anywhere near the shore,' said Puck, sounding disappointed, 'all the traffic with this coast would be with far smaller craft.'

It seemed to deflate their spirits slightly as the single piece of evidence they had deduced implied the message was about some ship making a continental crossing.

'Still, the locals involved round here would mostly have talked about boats, as it would be their own, they would be using back and forward; if they were talking 'ships,' it's still likely they meant a trip to France,' opined Maria valiantly. Tentative though it was, it seemed a plausible explanation, and as if to consolidate this positive thinking the girls parted and went home for tea, resolving to meet that evening at the pub: determined 'to have this out,' as Puck put it.

As they retraced their way back from the cliff top in the late afternoon sun the wide horizons gradually shrank as they made their way home to their drab little holiday cottage at the edge of the town. In many respects it was the ugly sister of their subterranean adventure, and it seemed particularly so this late in the day as the fading sun gave an austere khaki colour to the local brick of its old kaolin legacy. As with tonight over tea, they didn't dwell there and preferred the comeliness of the local pub which they'd been to each night. It hardly mattered in the grand scheme of things for what they had discovered in the mine still gave them a sense of owning an astonishing secret which they might or might not reveal one day to a benighted world entirely at their own discretion.

What's more, there was still the mystery of the wall's message, although as things currently stood, they'd be hard put to lift the scales from the eyes of any enquiring soul on that one.

The pub never changed very much, one night to the next: there was a pool of a dozen or so pensioners, always sat in their preferred seats, the darts players, punctilious as an atomic clock for the sanctity of their site and dimpled pint mugs, and early evening shoppers were regulars too, settling themselves down only where sufficient space was afforded for their loads. Meanwhile, tonight the lady of the house was supervising a change of keg in the cellar from a stool overlooking the stairs leading down, craning her neck over so that the cellarman could attend her peevish instructions.

As the evening wore on and the locals at the landlord's end of the bar became more animated it sometimes felt the pub was properly filling up, but half an hour later it would somehow lose the will, and numbers would just trickle away at a respectable rate until closing time.

Tonight, Maria and Ethyl were the first to arrive and Puck joined them ten minutes later; she sat with her half of scrumpy, picking at the dimples on the glass, as if distracted, then looked across towards the other two, like the cat that got the cream.

'I found something,' she said; 'it's a word we missed, and it could be important. Blanc!'

'I remember it!' said Maria, slightly miffed, 'we didn't miss it.' Ethyl looked as if she sided with Maria here, should culpability for the oversight prove to be an issue.

'No,' said Puck, 'I mean we missed the context where it fitted in; it referred to the ship.'

'White ship?' said Maria, 'How's that important?'

'Because' replied Puck, having drawn out the wee mouse, 'that was the name of the ship which in 1120 was crossing from France with Prince William aboard and which sank just outside the French port. He was the son of the English King Henry, and everyone drowned bar one sailor, including the Prince.'

'Like the Mary Rose,' volunteered Ethyl.

'That was Henry VIII's troop ship which sank off Portsmouth; this one was hundreds of years earlier. Henry I, I think, or rather his eldest son and heir Prince William.'

'So, you think these are swirling echoes we're hearing from all those years ago?' said Maria.

'Why not?' Puck replied, 'if you think about it, ten years is no more incredible than a thousand, or last week for that matter.'

'Maybe the wall's beginning a whispered documentary history of the millennium, like a sort of audio Venerable Bede,' said Ethyl, mediating her incredulity with the flourish of her prose.

'And you know all this how?' asked Maria.

'Backdated search engine,' admitted Puck.

'How does any of this help us make any sense of what's being said though?' remarked Maria, alert to the 'res' of the matter.

'Well, I think what we have here is a plan to kidnap and then murder Prince William,' said Puck emphatically; 'I know he would have drowned anyway, but they didn't know that at the time.'

'By whom?' asked Ethel, not so much disbelieving, as entirely ignorant of any 'dramatis personae' of early Norman England.

'The culprit,' said Puck, conscious that there was little she could manage of a Poirot-esque fanfare, 'has to be Stephen of Blois.'

It was just too hard to resist; like a spontaneous double act Maria's eyes met Ethyl's, and they high fived a joint: 'knew it all along!'

'I know, I know,' went Puck, aware she'd set herself up, but she was determined to remain didactic for the greater good of the mission.

'Henry I, the Prince's father, was King in England at the time with no other male heirs other than William, and if anything were to happen to him, who should then be next in line, but this Stephen of Blois, apart from Henry's daughter, who obviously didn't count.'

This assertion would perforce raise the hackles of any self-respecting sister, but as it might well be an unarguable C12th verity, Puck was able to continue:

'So, this must be some clandestine meeting held between Stephen and one or more assassins to kidnap and murder him before he can board this 'White Ship,' on its way back from France.'

'So why is it reaching us down an old mine in Cornwall?' asked Maria, quite reasonably.

Puck pursed her lips intently to answer Maria's query, barely a notch less than her epithet depicted as characteristic.

'My theory is that Stephen had come over to Cornwall especially, as it was a safer haven for him in which to organise the murder.'

'This is what we heard in the wall then is it?' said Maria, 'locked up for a thousand years from everyone except us.' Her tone was on the margins of a reawakening cynicism.

'None of us know how it's done,' answered Ethyl, in support of Puck's endeavour, 'but we all heard it.'

'And it fits,' re-joined Puck, still with some fruits of her research unpublished; 'the assassins must have intercepted him before the White Ship sailed and done him over in a ditch somewhere.

Apparently, it was packed to the rafters and left in the middle of the night when they were all still partying so probably no one missed him, while Stephen almost caught it himself, which would have been ironic, though in the end he decided not to. Anyway, he becomes King in 1435 when Henry, the Prince's father dies.' Puck thought she'd better can the donnish lecture at this point and instead appeal to more demotic sensibilities. 'Stephen and Matilda?' she said, looking up, 'it's famous because of all the turmoil of the reign, even I'd heard of them.'

Maria didn't seem to share Puck's appeal to some common-sense lore ruling over Stephen's hapless time as King but had nothing to add.

'What of Spartacus?' remarked Ethyl instead, 'we've forgotten all about him. He's totally out of it, a different time, place, everything.'

'Thrace,' repeated Maria, proudly, recalling the other fact which had emerged that had no bearing whatsoever on the twelfth century.

'That must have been the code name they had for the Prince,' said Puck confidently. 'It certainly fits in if you listen, probably an extra safety precaution: after all, walls have ears.'

An amusing note to end Puck's thesis satisfactorily subdued any further doubts in the ranks, conscious as they were that neither of them had any alternative to offer, and they were happy to leave it there. Ethyl's next remark perhaps adequately summarised the collective spirit:

'Well even though the case would be thrown out of court as seven pillars short of circumstantial, it will have to do for us, if only because we will never be sure one way or the other. Now, time for another m'dears,' and she pushed her dimpled glass far enough toward the middle of the table to leave neither of the pair opposite in any doubt that she saw the onus lay elsewhere.

But before there could be any response from the other two the landlord appeared in front of their table brandishing what looked like lottery tickets in his sizeable fist. As it was Friday night, he saw it as his prerogative to detach himself from his usual gathering of cronies at the end of the bar and make a break for freedom, despite the serious disruption to trade risked by handing responsibility over to his wife. So committed was he to this change in his normal routine that he even put on a tie for the occasion and left his tea cloth behind, though this may have had more to do with the very special event he was trying to sell, which only happened on this one particular week of the year.

'Can I interest you good ladies in tickets for tonight's recital?' he said cheerily, flapping them for effect. When he saw that the look on their faces was at least halfway to total bemusement, he took a pace back, extended his arm and flapped the tickets meaningfully at a poster behind the bar advertising the event.

'It's our Church Organ Master,' he revealed, 'he's famous-like in the whole of Cornwall, and every year at the end of Spring he gives a recital at the Hall down in the old town. Most of them codgers from here'll be going. Look in myself, if I get the chance.'

'When's it starts?' asked Puck, errant spirit of the three.

'Ten o'clock,' he replied merrily, made-up at such a bright response, 'go on, you'll enjoy it, only a pound each.'

Another flap, and he felt he'd surely delivered the prize.

'It's our last night,' went Maria plaintively, organ recitals clearly not part of any valedictory evening she had in mind.

'I don't know,' said Ethyl, on the fence, aware how lame 'I wanted to wash my hair' sounded, even as she said it.

'Oh, let's do it,' said Puck, smiling up at the landlord, who saw that if he added an 'only lasts an hour' at this stage, that that could nail it.

He was right, tickets and cash were exchanged over their table, and instead of abandoning them and rounding on the next victim, he dutifully remained to complete his pitching duties.

'The Old Hall's along near the bottom of the lane that goes down to the fishing harbour,' he said, 'it's the turning before the one to the beach that everyone uses.'

'It won't be deserted? will it,' asked Ethyl, suddenly feeling an enhanced fondness for the pub, notwithstanding the outlay of a pound.

'Or dark?' added Maria.

'Not at all,' replied the landlord lustily, for as scruples went, they didn't come much easier than these to allay. 'Light to near midnight this time of year in our part of the world; been some sort of recital there going way back.'

'Pagan times?' enquired Puck.

'Dare say,' he replied obligingly, 'anyway, there's a gas light at the end of the lane.'

With that, he pressed on to the shoppers, presumably with storage options available as his central selling point.

'Still time for another,' said Ethyl, resuming her thrust of the dimpled glass, and a quick time check, and synchronisation of watches began, while Puck's resistance weakened first in the general unreadiness to go to the bar.

At nine thirty the three girls left the pub and headed back to the road down to the sea, taking not the usual one to the beach, but the one leading to the old harbour, as instructed. It was less craggy and had fewer tight bends so they could see the outline of the sea way in front of them. No one had left the pub before them, and they couldn't see anyone ahead, which made them wonder about how popular the concert might prove to be, despite the landlord's puffery. As the lane straightened, the steep rocks to either side fell away and the small harbour appeared almost immediately in front of them, obviously long abandoned, its stonework cracked and wasted, its aged mooring facilities broken and rusted, and the only evidence that it had once had a fishing industry was a pair of decrepit wooden carcasses, which had presumably once been trawlers.

But the landlord had been correct in his interpretation of the solar year, there was indeed still plenty of light and as if to particularly solace Maria, where the lane joined the shoreline, there was indeed a streetlamp, burning bright as the evening star.

'Any sign of the old Hall?' said Ethyl, looking back the way they'd come.

'Nor concert-goers, nor anyone else since we turned down here,' said Puck, despondently.

There didn't even look as if there was anywhere promising to investigate; the lane gave out twenty yards beyond the lamp and the harbour was tucked into the edge of a wider bay, equally deserted, which edged round to the more picturesque beach on the near side, and an exposed and windswept strand of shingle and rock on the far one.

Then Maria turned her gaze back up the lane just in time to see a solitary pedestrian turn down a path they'd not noticed at the point where the cliff gave way into sand. They walked back and made the turn down the same path, walking single file as it led past the back of some old, dilapidated fisherman's cottages, though already the person in front of them had disappeared from view. This path, which had started out as neglected, became more and more dishevelled as they went on, until eventually it caused them to stop, firstly to clear bracken and twisted old branches out of the way, and second, to reconsider the wisdom of continuing. Of the three, Ethyl was most decided to go back and was about to make her opinion felt, when Puck, suddenly saying 'look,' stopped her.

'There,' and she pointed to a gap between two cottages, now overgrown with weeds, through which the spectre of the pedestrian had just made a fleeting appearance and was now heading jauntily towards what seemed to be a great wooden barn, lights blazing where you'd expect the hayloft to be, and humming away with a sound like some sort of energy pulse, audible even from their distance.

Puck led the way through the final obstacle of entwined tree limbs and thick foliage, which somehow hadn't seemed to trouble the person ahead of them, and into the old cottage's side-entrance. This now continued into the remains of what must have been an old settlement; a sand strewn narrow street, a deserted village store, and some sheds, with collapsed prepping benches and rusted bins below, where fishermen's wives gutted and boned the catch; and a sign above the store, faded and engrained with sand, which read: 'Adelin Square.'

The wooden Hall was ahead of them now and though it had probably once been some sort of storehouse attached to the old fishing port it was clear from the size of the edifice that this must indeed be the venue for the recital, albeit still short of anything suggesting an attendance, other than the phantom they had been following. Not any last-minute stragglers like themselves, no market movers or touts outside, cleaning up on the entertainment extravaganza of the year, nor even officials manning the door and checking tickets of honest subscribers; not even a door, apparently.

It faced seawards and was lit only at the upper level, which made it look rather like a giant beacon, set as it was in this deserted part of the coast, with all its lower level in darkness.

They walked up to the facade then round the corner, where the roll and lick of the waves revealed its exposure towards the sea and from which a crude portal extended outward, while a cursory investigation beyond this point revealed no other way in.

There was an old plaid curtain suspended by a brass rod at the entrance to the inner sanctum. Puck drew it far enough to one side to see in, but the lack of light within meant nothing much was visible, so she slipped in, followed by the other two. Immediately, the electronic hum they had heard from outside was intensified, then, once their eyes had adjusted, what they saw was a great space laid out as an auditorium, with rows of wooden tip-up chairs laid out either side of a central aisle. This leads up to the stage, of minimal elevation, but more than wide enough to accommodate the splendid organ which stood fore-square. Such light as there was, was provided from half a dozen Osram bulbs on each wall, of barely outhouse wattage, and a low-grade electric chandelier halfway down the aisle, with a pair of hurricane lamps, which looked like they'd been swiped from the nearest roadworks, illuminating the stage. If the light from the hayloft served any purpose it was quite superfluous to the evening's entertainment, as the two floors were entirely separate, while the great size of the Hall only served to emphasise its almost total emptiness, just a handful of other brave souls having settled as far away from each other as they could manage.

Ethyl checked her watch; it was a few minutes past ten. 'This place must have been used as a church at some point,' she said, 'look at all those bays they've screened off up each side, they must have been separate chapels.'

'That's true,' said Puck, ' and all those bare indents halfway up the wall, seven each side, they could have been used for Stations of the Cross.'

'That's Catholic, isn't it? I would have thought they disappeared round here after the Reformation.'

'Maybe they did,' replied Puck.

'This is a waste of time,' said Maria, 'there's no one here, certainly no one from the pub.'

'Give it a couple of more minutes,' said Ethyl compliantly, 'then we go.'

'Don't you think that humming's weird?' said Puck. 'It seems to be all around us, just a drone; like a sound system has been turned on with nothing to play.'

Suddenly a man appeared from the wings, walked across the stage and bowed theatrically, possibly for the benefit of those at the back, like Maria, Ethyl and Puck. He was dressed sombrely in a dark grey suit, white shirt and black tie; you couldn't see his face properly, so he would have to remain ageless, all you could make out was a receding hairline of lank greasy hair which hung scruffily over the back of his collar when he turned his back, which he now did as he took up his place at the organ, to applause which was several purls short of a ripple, looking a bit like one of those stencils from the original 'Sketches by Boz.'

The organ now blasted into life with a grand C major chord that demanded instant attention.

It was mighty loud, majestic, and the canon sounded more religious than ceremonial; but after the initial brio it settled into something more technically complex, with waves of harmonies starting to undulate from deep within, as if some great backward brute of an Edwardian church organ could synth and mix. A low choral strain now sounded, emerging from the harmonic scales, evolving all the while, now rising above, now subsumed by the next thematic layer from the organ.

Distinct vocal sounds added their own harmonies, which caused the girls to instinctively look up and behind them for a glimpse of the choir. But there was nothing except old rafters and struts supporting the roof.

'Somehow,' said Puck leaning across to make herself heard, 'that organ is producing those same freaky sounds we heard in the mine. It's hard to explain; it's completely original, yet the harmonies it's mixing sound just the same.'

'There's a choir coming from somewhere,' said Ethyl, 'and it's getting louder.'

In fact, the sound of the choir had now reached such a pitch and intensity that it had become the focal point of the work, with the organ weaving in and out of the sung text or rising to its crescendo as the choir reached its fullest refrains. It was now apparent that what was playing was some sort of oratorio or mass; in any event the Hall was reverting to its former role, as the words being sung were clearly devotional, and if the orchestral harmonies evoked those of the pit's inner sanctum, here they were augmented by prayers sung from either wing, high as the attic for treble descants, low as the bare wooden wainscoting, splintered by age and semi-devoured by woodworm, for the bass. The hissing and whispering had now dispersed, to be replaced by a wonderful clarity, as if the piety of the work somehow had its own immanent self-reverence. The organ now played a more measured, supportive role as it was the words of the prayers and their sequence which summoned the spirits.

Kyrie Eleison, Sanctus,

Hosanna in Excelsis,

Agnus Dei,

In Paradisum.

The text of the Requiem Mass.

At the end, no one quite knew what to do; the atmosphere was electric in the sudden quiet and the organist remained seated. It seemed as if everybody was waiting for someone else to begin applauding, conscious of how conspicuous they would be and half hoping that the only player in evidence would scuttle off as quickly as he had appeared.

Instead, he stood to face the audience, bowed again, then said: 'Thank you very much for attending on this solemn occasion, it means so much to us all. My name is Richard Adelin.'

And with that he did scuttle off, while the score or so in attendance were belatedly shamed into another perfunctory round of applause.

In fact, embarrassment was the dominant feeling all round; it had been ever since it became clear the concert anticipated would be a fiasco, and lasted all the way through to the end, with half a dozen little clusters of reluctant sojourners, utterly uncomprehending, and dead set on making their escape. Fortunately, some enterprising caretaker or other had opened another door leading to the old settlement where the streetlight shone so brightly that everybody was reminded of the lateness of the hour.

Most elected to leave by this route, as it was somehow easier to stagger departure times: Perhaps the lamp brought renewed heart, some assurance that the reverse in existential polarity they'd experienced that evening had been but a blip. Only the three girls left by the door to the seashore.

'What did you make of that?' said Ethyl, probably the most sceptical of the three, but stunned to the quick, nonetheless.

'There's your answer,' replied Maria, referring to an extremely inconspicuous notice, beyond yellow with age, pinned to the inside of the door.

Tonight: Requiem Mass for William Adelin. RIP.

www.ingramcontent.com/pod-product-compliance
Lightning Source LLC
Chambersburg PA
CBHW070550180626
46817CB00005B/1779